"There's no way you can force me to marry you!"

Ria's eyes flashed fire at the tall, menacing figure of her *host*. "You will never force yourself on me!"

"Ah, I regret it appears I failed to make my proposal absolutely clear," Vitor said, mocking her with a slight formal bow.

"My purpose in offering you marriage is to prevent your guardian from exploiting you and, incidentally, making your life a misery. It is not my intention to exercise the usual rights of a husband in the bedroom."

Ria stared in disbelief at her captor.

"Your virginity will remain safe in my custody as it has for the past six years at your religious retreat. That will be my revenge against Gustavo."

Revenge? Ria thought wildly. Revenge for what? And what did this madman mean about preventing Gustavo from exploiting her?

D0039801

Angela Wells left the bustling world of media marketing and advertising to marry and start a family in a suburb of London. Writing started out as a hobby, and she uses backgrounds she knows well from her many travels for her books. Her ambitions, she says, in addition to writing many more romances, are to visit Australia, pilot a light aircraft and own a word-processor.

Books by Angela Wells

HARLEQUIN ROMANCE
2790—SWEET POISON
2844—MOROCCAN MADNESS
2903—DESPERATE REMEDY

Fortune's Fool
Angela Wells

Harlequin Books

TORONTO • NEW YORK • LONDON
AMSTERDAM • PARIS • SYDNEY • HAMBURG
STOCKHOLM • ATHENS • TOKYO • MILAN

Original hardcover edition published in 1987
by Mills & Boon Limited

ISBN 0-373-02921-7

Harlequin Romance first edition July 1988

CHAPTER ONE

THE car had stopped. Ria was conscious of distant conversation, a sharp command, a voice raised in alter-
cation as she struggled to awaken from the deep sleep
which had claimed her.

It was hardly surprising she had nodded off in the
back of the large limousine sent to collect her from São
Paolo airport. Having spent most of the previous night
awake in her simple convent bedroom, filled with an excitement tinged with apprehension at the unknown future
awaiting her, she had still been tired but unable to sleep
on the two-hour flight from Salvador.

Once installed in the luxurious chauffeur-driven car
her guardian had sent to bring her to his villa on the
outskirts of Campinas she had succumbed to her weariness, aided by the late afternoon heat of the sultry
Brazilian summer.

'*Vossa Excelencia* . . . will you do me the honour of
alighting?'

It was the authoritative timbre of the deep male voice
as much as the feel of unyielding fingers on her arm that
pierced through the remnants of her slumber, bringing
Ria back to reality with a start.

'I'm sorry . . .' The apology sprang easily from her lips
as her free arm rose with unconscious vanity to smooth
the stray tendrils of blonde hair away from her neck,
tucking them into the neat chignon from which they'd
escaped, before allowing herself to be helped from the
car. A thrill of expectation surged through her at the
prospect of seeing the house where she was about to play

the role of housekeeper and companion to the man who
had taken her from the slums of São Paolo.

Stepping down and looking around she realised for
the first time that something was wrong. Very wrong.
The car had stopped...or been stopped?...on a narrow
roadway between rising hills to the left and forest to the
right. There was no sign of any civilisation at all—let
alone a country villa. After her first wild glance around,
Ria knew she would find none.

Fighting to control the terror which momentarily
blocked her throat, her frightened eyes absorbed the
scene around her. A few yards down the road the driver
of the car was standing, his back pressed hard against
the rising rocks, each arm firmly held by two men casually dressed in denim trousers and checked shirts, their
lower faces covered by cotton scarves.

Slowly she forced herself to turn towards the man
beside her as his hand tightened warningly beneath the
elbow.

It was the first time she had looked at him and she
felt her mouth drop open in surprise. She had expected
he, too, would have his face hidden—like the other two
bandits—because that, surely, was what they were. But
the dark eyes that met her own were intensely beautiful
in a face that she would remember for the rest of her
life: a long oval bisected by the heavy, shapely bar of
jet eyebrows beneath which his breathtakingly brilliant
eyes were surveying her from pools of shade. His nose
was straight and strong above the mouth of a sinner—
firm and sensuous, generous and passionate, the chin
rounded beneath the groove of the lower lip, but jutting
and hard.

No deviant youth, this. She was looking at a fully
grown specimen of manhood, probably no more than
thirty. In the seconds her appraisal took, Ria stood

transfixed as if she were staring at a hitherto unknown species. In a way she was, she allowed. For what experience of men did she have after all? Father Gonzales who was the convent's priest, her elderly guardian and the defeated, hopeless inhabitants of the *favela* where she had lived with her mother until the latter's death.

Her gaze drifted upwards embracing well shaped ears flat against the personable head, thick black hair like a field of jet above the broad forehead.

'Will you know me again when we meet, *namorada*?' The corners of his mouth lifted as the amusement in his voice reflected the smile in his eyes.

'Yes...no...I...' Ria fought down her fear, casting anxious eyes towards the captured driver. He appeared unhurt, and there were no signs that the bandits were carrying guns. She assumed the men must have waved the car down. She had no idea where they were but as they had obviously left the main road she guessed they couldn't be too far from her final destination.

If only she could bluff her way out—persuade them to take the car maybe and leave her alone. It shouldn't be too long a walk to safety.

'I don't have any money on me.' She drew herself up to her full height, a graceful five foot six inches, but the man beside her dwarfed her.

'What makes you think I want your money, *namorada*?'

'Isn't that what bandits usually want?' Ria tossed him a challenging look as her initial terror began to ebb. The casual use of the endearment with which he addressed her somehow soothed her, although conversely the familiarity irked her.

A sable eyebrow lifted. 'What makes you think I'm a bandit?'

'Well, I don't think you're selling ice-cream!' The retort came tartly to her lips—to be regretted instantly. She must keep her temper! After six years of convent discipline she ought to have learned that lesson—apart from chastity, docility and obedience were the two greatest female virtues she had been taught.

Quickly placatory, she turned limpid blue eyes to regard her captor pleadingly. Obviously he was the leader of the small band, the other two members staying with their prisoner practically out of earshot.

'I haven't anything of value on me, honestly.' She stared unblinkingly at his watchful face, content that she spoke the truth. Her only luggage was a suitcase containing the clothes she had worn at the convent—dull, simple modest dresses and even duller underwear!

'You think that concerns me when I hold the most valuable prize of all in my hand at this moment?' His soft laugh riveted her senses, as his arm left her elbow to slide around her shoulders.

Fool that she was! His game was kidnap, not robbery. Ria's brain clicked over with computer speed. This had been no random hold-up. Somehow this arrogant stranger had known of her journey and had planned all along to abduct her. Gustavo Veloso was a rich man with his fingers in many pies—industrial as well as political, that at least she knew about him although she was totally ignorant of the details. And she was his ward. For six years he had had her educated at his own expense. A feeling of nausea overwhelmed her. What price had they put on her head, she wondered angrily, knowing that somehow she must try to thwart their plans.

'Me...a prize?' She feigned innocence. 'I can assure you if you believe that then you're the only person who would put a value on me.'

Even to her own ears her laugh sounded forced.

'Such modesty.' His mouth curled into a smile revealing even white teeth. 'But you lie, Maria Bernardi!' The smile uncurled, died. 'Gustavo Veloso has waited six years for this day, and has vested a good deal of money to achieve his ends.'

'Maria Bernardi? You thought I was Maria?' Courage gave her the strength to oppose him. Then, as she saw his frown line the clear skin of his forehead, she continued in a rush of words. 'Poor Maria, the day before she was due to come here she developed this awful rash. Well, you see Senhor Veloso was depending on her to be his hostess at this party he's giving...' Ria's heart was thundering as she improvised wildly. 'So he had to send to São Paolo to get someone to take her place and...'

As a story it was so full of holes it would have been a miracle if the man at her side had fallen for it, and Ria felt almost grateful when he stopped her in full spate before she ran out of lies.

'Not Maria Bernardi, eh?' A swift movement of his free hand and he was tugging at the fastenings of her chignon. 'Tell me another woman in this mighty country who has hair to rival the silver beauty of the sands at Copacabana.'

Ria gasped as her unloosed tresses fell in a swirl of movement round her heart-shaped face. Attempting to take a step backwards she found herself pulled even closer to her captor whose previous good temper now seemed to have been submerged in a pulsating wave of anger.

'Tell me,' he insisted, his voice burning darkly in the vibrant stillness surrounding them. 'What other woman is there with the pale eyes and skin of the north and the warm voluptuous curves of the south?'

A prisoner in his arms, Ria could do nothing to prevent his hard cruel fingers from reaching for her breasts, weighing their heavy beauty in his palm while the heat of his hand seared through the light cotton dress she wore.

'Don't touch me!' she instructed wrathfully. She had been taught that her body was the sacred temple of her soul, to be touched intimately only within the sacrament of marriage. The rough male fingers so masterfully intent were an insult, making her break out in a sweat of shame and despair.

As if she hadn't spoken his hand remained in place for an agonising few seconds, while Ria stared down at it as if hypnotised. She had expected to see the hand of a labourer, square-fingered and broad, but she had been wrong. Tanned and solid, yes. But the fingers she resented so deeply were long and slender, the nails smooth and kempt. His clothes too, she noticed, although simple were good, the trousers well fitting to his lean long thighs and flat hips, the shirt the finest cotton, the chain lying against his strong neck gold. Obviously there was a fortune to be made from this evil trade of body-snatching, she thought angrily.

'So...' Dark eyes regarded her intently. 'Show me another woman who has a waist as slender as Maria Bernardi.' With firm deliberation his hand moved to illustrate his words. 'Or hips as firm yet soft.'

'All right!' Ria could have wept with frustration. 'I *am* Maria Bernardi! Now, will you take your hands off me!'

He obeyed her slowly with the air of one who was following his own inclinations anyway.

'Good.' A curt nod of his head approved her confession. 'Believe me, there's no need for you to be afraid. There's been a slight change of plan, but none that need alarm you. As you've no doubt realised, you won't be going to the destination you anticipated. Instead you'll be *my* guest.'

'And what about the driver?' Ria glanced anxiously down the road. 'What plans have you made for him? Will you hold him a captive—or is he going to deliver the ransom note?'

She couldn't hide the anxiety in her voice. Hopefully the man would be released. His captors were masked and it seemed the man at her side hadn't been that close to him to be recognised again. Yet *she* would be able to recognise him...anywhere. The thought made her grow cold. What was her future worth when she could identify him?

'Don't be concerned about him. He'll be fine. After we've left he'll be put back into the car, which will be disabled and parked off the road. Hopefully he'll be discovered within a couple of hours with no harm done except possibly to his pride.'

So the car was staying. Presumably such an expensive vehicle would be readily identifiable and not worth the risk of stealing. But where was she going to be taken, and how?

The man beside her must have read her thoughts. 'As for you and me, I thought you'd like a change from the stuffiness of a car. We'll be continuing our journey on horseback.' He indicated the stretch of forest land. 'Besides being a pleasant exercise, it's a much safer way of travelling to avoid detection.'

'But I can't ride!'

As soon as the words had left her mouth Ria was furious with herself. She could have tried to elude him, couldn't she? She might even have managed to gallop away from him and escape!

'Oh, no, you couldn't!' White teeth gleamed again as he read her thoughts. Was she really so transparent? 'Do you really think I'd be stupid enough to give you your own mount? Oh, no my sweet *namorada*—we ride together!' Ignoring the look of hatred she flashed him, he took her firmly by the arm. 'Come, we've wasted enough time already. Even though we've put up a temporary road block to prevent other traffic from chancing on us, I've no wish to put too much faith in luck.'

Ria allowed herself to be led for three paces before stopping to voice a still present concern. 'The driver...he...you...'

'He won't be hurt in any way—I give you my word.'

The assurance came swiftly and seemed sincere. Ria supposed she would have to accept it. Bandit or not, when a Brazilian gave his word he inevitably kept it. It was a matter of pride and had nothing to do with morals, only self-respect, and it was clear the man whose invitation she was being forced to accept had plenty of that!

'Wait!' He stopped abruptly. '*Meu Deus*, I nearly forgot!'

Before she knew what was happening, let alone had the opportunity to protest, Ria found herself gathered closely into her captor's arms. Struggling angrily as she felt the hard contours of his body pressing against her own soft curves, she tried to fight him off, only to find her face held and lifted. There was a devilish gleam in his dark eyes as he lowered his head and kissed her with passionate persistence.

As his tongue teased her lips, she fought like a jungle cat for her freedom, hands clawing at his back, nails piercing the thin veil of his shirt.

'You peasant!' She spat the words out at him just as soon as he allowed her sovereignty over her own mouth.

'Hush!' He countered her attack briefly as she seethed in silence. 'You are more peasant than I—though why you should deem such a state dishonourable escapes me.'

'Don't mock me!' Ria was beyond fear now. 'I can understand crimes committed through the scourge of poverty—although I don't condone them. But to use force to abuse a woman physically—and one who is your prisoner, totally outnumbered by your gang—is despicable and ignoble. It makes you worse than an animal!'

'My dear girl...' Her flow of words was halted in midstream by the man's quiet interception. 'I haven't the slightest idea of abusing you, or of holding you to ransom.'

There was a deadly earnestness about the dark face so close to her own. Ria felt her heart thunder with the strength and intensity of the beat of the samba. An exciting, vibrating rhythm that stirred the blood and fed the emotions.

'Then why...?'

For a moment she thought he wasn't going to answer. Then he sighed.

'I was going to tell you when we reached the place where we're going. But you might as well know now.'

He paused.

Ria's mouth was shockingly dry, her legs were weak, barely supporting her. Dear heavens! If he wasn't going to rape her or hold her to ransom, what else was there? Unless he was insane—a madman escaped from some asylum.

'Go on,' she whispered, steeling herself for the answer.

'Because I mean to marry you. By this time tomorrow you'll be my wife.'

CHAPTER TWO

Of course he had been joking with her. Ria sank down gingerly into the most comfortable-looking chair in the simply furnished room which appeared to be the main living-room of the farmhouse to which she had been taken after her ordeal on horseback.

Every bone in her body ached! Even the hot bath she had been invited to take had done little to alleviate the soreness of her thighs. Obliged to sit astride, held embarrassingly close to her tormentor, she had been torn between her dislike of feeling his body so near to her own and her terror at finding herself perched so high and insecurely above the ground. Dear heavens! She had never realised how tall a horse was until that horrifying moment she had been swept up into the saddle!

Perhaps his joke about marriage had been intended to take her mind off her ordeal? It had certainly given her something to think about during the seemingly interminable ride through the forest and subsequent grassland. Common sense told her the idea of marriage was absurd because there was no way her captor would benefit from such a bizarre alliance.

She might be Gustavo Veloso's ward but that didn't mean she was his heir. Even if she had been, all he had to do was change his will. No, there had to be another reason and doubtless she would learn what it was in due course. At least she wasn't alone with him. An involuntary shudder passed through Ria's tired body. If he were to be proved deranged there must surely be others here who would be sane—and who would help her?

16

As far as she had been able to make out, the farmhouse was on the outskirts of a cotton plantation. She had glimpsed outbuildings that probably housed the workers and heard a child cry briefly before being soothed into silence.

Then there was the woman called Floriana—a *mestizo*, her mixed Indian and European blood clearly indicated on her dark bony face, the lines which creased her skin telling their own story of heavy labour and hardship.

It had been Floriana to whom she had been delivered on her forced arrival. She had been dirty and distressed, her heart fluttering like a trapped bird as she strove to hide the depth of her panic while her dark-browed companion had summoned the *mestizo* woman, ordering that his guest should be given refreshment and a bath.

'I am clean enough, *senhor*!' Ria had retorted tartly, ignoring the travel stains that streaked her face and hands, and extremely unwilling to disrobe under the same roof as the arrogant bandit who gave his orders with such careless authority.

With expressive eyebrows he questioned her short statement, passing impertinent eyes from her crown to her toes, shrugging his broad shoulders at her discomfiture.

'Your muscles are going to be stiff enough as it is— and not only where they were in contact with the horse.' A brief lowering of his eyelids disguised the amusement she guessed lurked in the depths of those dark eyes. 'Believe me, I've never felt such tension in any woman's body. Holding you in place was like sharing the saddle with a plaster saint!'

'I'm surprised you have even a nodding acquaintance with such holy statues.' Swiftly Ria mocked him. And as for feeling tension in a woman's body...when she was released from this unlikely prison she would make

it her business to ensure it was a long, long time before
he even saw a female again—let alone held one as close
as she had been on that infamous journey.

'And I'm surprised your gift for repartee hasn't long
since been squashed by the good sisters at the convent.
A sharp tongue like yours must have earned its owner
many a penance over the years.'

Ria had flushed, too honest to deny the truth of his
assertion. In the early days of her schooling she had
always been in trouble. During the period of her mother's
last illness she had been forced to survive by her own
wits. Too frail to protect herself physically, it had been
her verbal skills that had won her a place in the pack of
children with which she'd hunted—sifting through the
city rubbish dumps—rummaging in the street markets—
for a few morsels of sustenance for both of them, not
realising at the time just how sick her mother was. She
had lifted angry vulnerable eyes to the wicked face that
surveyed her with sardonic humor.

'Perhaps I wasn't a model pupil.'

But she'd learned—oh, yes she'd learned! Not through
fear but gratitude. Gustavo Veloso had given her a stake
in the future and she had been determined not to disappoint him, even although to her shame she had never
been able to regard him with the affection his action had
merited. Despite his charity towards her he had remained a remote, almost sinister figure to her young eyes.

Her face had been taut with indignation as she'd lifted
her fair head with an inborn haughtiness. 'But I never
stooped to crime. I never did anything I was ashamed
of!'

Staring at the whitewashed walls, Ria felt her body
grow warm all over. What a fool she had been to taunt
him! With one blow of his powerful hand he could have
sent her spinning across the room. Yet all he had done

was give a short guffaw of laughter—almost as if her spirit pleased him.

'Have your bath, *menina*, don't worry about prying eyes. Floriana will serve you if you wish it, but no man will dare to step across the threshold unless I permit it, and as for myself...'

He had paused long enough to make her catch her breath in apprehension before finishing the sentence. '...I have work to do outside. We shall talk later when we are both refreshed and less tired.'

Perhaps, Ria wondered now, trying unsuccessfully to settle her weary bones, if she had allowed Floriana to minister to her in the bath, she might have been able to engage the woman in conversation, find out more about the place to which she had been brought... and the man who strode through it as if he owned it. But she had lived too long in an environment where the body had been disciplined to the needs of the soul to be happy about exposing her nakedness to anyone—even a member of her own sex. She had been taught how to dress and undress without ever being totally naked, although struggling beneath her voluminous cotton nightdress to divest herself of her serviceable briefs and simple bra she had sometimes had to fight the desire to strip everything off just for the pure fun of it!

As it was, her exchange of words with the *mestizo* woman had been minimal, adding nothing to the paucity of information she had already gleaned. So she had resigned herself to making the most of the warm bath and the long, cool drink of fruit juice with which she had been served.

Now it seemed all she could do was wait to find out the truth about the day's disturbing—and criminal— events.

"My apologies for keeping you waiting.'

The door had opened silently while Ria had still been deep in thought, to reveal the tall, broad-shouldered form of her kidnapper. He, too, had bathed or showered, she noticed seeing the dampness lying like beads on his sable head, but unlike herself, he was wearing fresh clothes; the tough denim trousers replaced by dark fawn linen and the plain shirt having given way to a beautifully styled chocolate and fawn stretch shirt that eased over a hard muscled chest.

He looked irritatingly handsome and devastatingly civilised—which just went to show how misleading appearances could be. Not only could the Devil cite scripture—it appeared he could also dress like an angel!

'And *my* apologies for not changing for dinner.' There was a sweet sarcasm in her gentle voice which he certainly hadn't missed as he lounged down in a facing chair. 'Unfortunately I was waylaid by brigands on the way and they made off with everything in the world I own.'

Cool eyes scrutinised her angry face. 'If what you're wearing at the present time is an example of your total wardrobe—then believe me you're well rid of it.'

'A convent school is hardly a fashion house,' Ria thrust back, only too well aware of the truth of his remark. 'But there were other items in the case I treasured—my rosary and the Bible my mother gave me.'

'Which will be returned to you, I swear it!' There was a harsh venom in his voice which reminded her that this was no gentleman sitting opposite her. 'What did you think would happen to them? That they'd appear in some street market somewhere with a price on them?'

'A reasonable supposition, surely.' Ria refused to be cowed by his anger. 'Everything else you've done today has been outside the law, why should I credit you with a conscience?'

Even as the words left her mouth Ria wondered what on earth she was doing sitting there discussing ethics with the handsome villain who held her future in his hands. Whatever happened she mustn't let the fact that he had treated her with courtesy since her arrival in his domain influence her. Beneath the veneer of culture lay a ruthless spirit. If it were otherwise she wouldn't be here now.

'Outside the law?' It was a pleasant smile that greeted her accusation. 'Well, perhaps in the strictest sense, *meu amor*, but ritual elopement and seduction have long been accepted as a virile lover's demonstration of "machismo", and I can't see the law taking any interest in the matter—particularly as your abduction is to be so quickly regularised by marriage.'

Golden lashes devoid of make-up flew upwards to search the sombre features opposite her for any sign that he was teasing her for some cruel pleasure of his own. Shaken by the seriousness of his expression, Ria could only stumble out her horror in broken sentences.

'But we're not lovers. I don't know you... I've never seen you before. I don't even know your name. Please...' She made a valiant effort to swallow the lump in her throat as her nerves knotted in a cold hard fear. 'Please don't joke with me. You must know what you're proposing is impossible. My guardian would never give his consent. He wants me to be with him, act as his hostess...' She floundered to a stop.

The first time he had said he meant to marry her she hadn't believed him. Now, although she knew it was impossible, she no longer doubted his own strength of purpose to make her his wife.

'Listen to me, Ria.' His voice, firm and masterful, broke the sound of her rapid breath. 'You are called Ria, are you not?'

'Yes.' She nodded. She'd been named Frances Maria Bernardi, the first and last names after her father—the handsome blond Englishman who had loved and then left her mother without sanctifying their union, the man whom her mother had continued to love until the very day of her death fourteen years after their last parting, always believing he would return to claim her and his daughter.

She looked at her captor's face with icy eyes, her chin raised proudly. He had certainly done his homework well.

'Well then, Ria, there are many things I have to tell you, but first, since we are to be man and wife you should certainly know my name. Allow me to present myself.' He stood up sweeping her a mock bow. 'Vitor Antonio Gregorio Fortunato.'

'Vitor Fortunato.' Ria allowed her disdain to show in the curl of her lovely mouth as she repeated the syllables. Somehow the name suited him.

'You've heard of me?'

Did she detect a flicker of pleasure in the question? Firmly she shook her head. 'Never,' she told him shortly. 'Should I have?'

'It was always possible.' He dismissed her non-recognition with a quick movement of one capable hand.

Ria clasped her own hands tightly together. The fact of his notoriety gave her little cause for comfort. 'Would recognising your name make it any more likely I'd understand your insistence on making me your wife?'

'Possibly,' he allowed tersely. 'Because you'd also learn there is a deep and long-lasting hatred existing between Gustavo Veloso and myself and therefore believe me when I told you I will stop at nothing until I've taken from him the one thing he cannot replace with money— his secret fantasy—the priceless pearl he has kept closed in the oyster until he could produce it to an admiring and respectful audience.'

There was a burning fanaticism on Vitor's strong face, a powerful surge of emotion in the harsh voice.

'You would know I won't rest until I've taken from Gustavo Veloso the one possession he treasures above all else, placed it beyond his reach and crushed for ever his long-held dream.'

As the burning wave of words washed over her, leaving her pale and trembling, Ria didn't need him to finish his explanation, could only stare at him entranced by the passion and pain that contorted his strong features as he confirmed what she had already understood.

'*You, menina*. You are the prize he's been gloating over these past years while his wife lay critically ill in a clinic and he offered up public prayers for her reprieve. *You*, my angel, carefully selected for your beauty, kept from the company of men, trained in womanly tasks until the day he should become a widower and could bring you publicly to his side as his new wife.'

He moved closer to her, stooping to lift her chin as she cowered away from his mouth.

'The day I meet Veloso face to face with you on my arm—the exquisite Senhora Fortunato—is the day I shall have claimed a major debt!'

'Senhor Fortunato.' Ria's dry lips stumbled on his name so eager was she to disillusion him. 'You're making a dreadful mistake. Senhor Veloso is my guardian, not my prospective husband! He's—well, he's sixty-five if he's a day.' Her anxious eyes invited his agreement, fruitlessly.

'He saved you from a life of poverty for a mere whim? Sent you away to school out of the goodness of his heart?' Vitor's sneer roused her latent anger.

'Yes, yes, he did! After my mother's death I was taken in by one of her friends. I used to call her Aunt Luisa. She lived in one room in a tenement building.' She frowned, recalling the tiny room barely large enough for one, let alone two. 'Then one day shortly after I'd arrived she took me to the big house where she worked in the kitchen and introduced me to Senhor Veloso—the owner.'

'And?' Vitor's expression gave nothing away.

Ria shrugged her shoulders. 'He was very kind to me— told me he had once known my mother and in her memory he was prepared to have me properly educated. He told me his wife was in bad health and would be unable to carry out her normal social and domestic duties, and that he was prepared to give me the status of his ward and to have me trained in a convent so that when the time came for me to leave I could take over the duties of his housekeeper and hostess.' Somehow she had to convince the vengeful man looming over her that he was appallingly mistaken. She choked back the sudden lump in her throat. 'I don't think Luisa really wanted to part with me and I was certainly very scared, but she persuaded me it was a marvellous opportunity for me to make something of myself...' Her voice trailed away into silence as she recalled that first meeting with the man who was to change the direction of her life. There had been some indefinable quality about him that had touched her spine with an icy finger. Some sense of foreboding that had made her want to fling herself into Luisa's arms and beg her not to agree. Yet to have refused the offer would have placed an almost impossible burden on the woman at her side.

'You innocent little fool!' It was the growl of a monster as Vitor hauled Ria to her feet, pushing her across the room to where a mirror hung against the wall. 'Look in there and tell me that villain saw only the penniless daughter of a woman he'd once known!'

Trying to avert her head, Ria found a firm hand wound in her long hair twisting painfully so she had no option but to obey.

'Your so-called guardian never had a charitable thought in his head since birth, *meu amor*. He looked at you and saw what any man would see—an uncommon beauty, a fairness of face and form that would tempt the Devil himself. He saw a child with the potential of great beauty and he lusted after her, just as he spent his days lusting after less virtuous ladies on the sleazy streets of Rio and São Paolo while his wife lay on her death bed.'

'You know a lot about it!' Ria challenged his information, her tear-bright eyes meeting his eyes in the mirror.

'Because I made it my business to find out,' came the quick answer. 'Oh, he kept his deviant behaviour well hidden from his friends and colleagues, and his women were too scared to betray him. Gradually I built up a dossier against him but there was nothing powerful enough to wound him as I intended to. Until I discovered your existence, *menina*. Until I found out he'd come across a waif from the *favela*, paying for her to be turned into a gracious lady out of his own pocket and keeping the fact so quiet he seldom spared the time to visit her.'

'He was busy.' Quickly Ria sprang to her guardian's defence.

'Busy protecting his reputation,' Vitor agreed grimly. 'He wanted to be seen as a Christian family man, honest, sincere and virtuous. None of which he is. The last thing he wanted to leak out was the fact he was already grooming an understudy for his wife who lay suffering in some expensive but remote clinic totally unaware of your existence.'

His fingers in Ria's mane of hair loosened, and he stood gazing at her broodingly as she smoothed down the havoc he had caused.

'His first marriage was for money. His wife was a plain woman nine years his senior, but her father owned a large coffee plantation. Now he has built another fortune on the backs of the poor, and this time he means to enjoy the physical pleasure of a beautiful and virtuous woman so long denied him. He was only waiting for his wife to die before bringing you back to take her place.' He paused then added with drawling deliberation, 'Two weeks ago she finally obliged him.'

'It's not true.' Eyes widening in a face grown suddenly pale, Ria dared to call him a liar. If Senhora Veloso had really died why hadn't she been told? The least she could have done would have been to send some flowers, even if their cost had been met from the small allowance her guardian had made her.

'No?' He accepted her accusation with comparative calm. 'My dear girl, you're what—nineteen?' Then, as she nodded, 'An age when very many girls are married and even mothers—yet you have only just been permitted to leave the sanctuary of school! Surely I don't have to make the facts any clearer? You were being kept in purdah until the happy day when Veloso was released from his marriage vows. Unfortunately for him, fate and the excellent drugs Senhora Veloso was given kept him waiting for his fulfilment much longer than he'd expected!'

Ria stared at Vitor's passive face, trying to control the nervous tremors that shivered through her body.

'You're mad!' she choked, shaking her head desperately trying to clear her confusion. 'Whatever grudge you've got against my guardian, it's nothing to do with me. I can't be forced into marriage—either by you or him—even if I believed that was his intention—which I don't!'

'Don't be too complacent. If Veloso threatens to throw you out unless you obey him, you'll have nothing. How long do you think you'd last in São Paolo with no clothes and no money? How long before you were forced to sell your body to feed your stomach? How long before you were back in the gutter he raised you from?'

For one moment she hesitated. Suppose, just suppose what he had said was true? This time there would be no Luisa to help her. Like so many women of her class and generation her mother's friend had been totally illiterate. In the early days Ria had sent her postcards with a simple message hoping she would get someone to read them to her. The only reply she ever received was from an unknown woman simply saying that Luisa Ferreira was no longer at that address. Resolutely she turned her back on her fears.

'That's a chance I'm going to take, because I think you're lying!'

Ria saw his face flush a dark angry red but the adrenalin was mounting in her veins and she was going to have her say. 'What about you? There's no way you can force me to marry you. I won't. And there's nothing you can do about it!'

For a moment of stretching time they faced each other like animals squaring up for a fight to the death. It was Vitor who relaxed first.

Taking Ria's trembling arm he led her gently towards the window. In the distance she could make out the figure of labourers returning to their homes on the plantation.

'You see those men?' he asked quietly.

Silently Ria nodded, a strange foreboding draining the blood from her face. Vitor seemed so sure of himself, so certain he held the whip hand.

Softly he continued speaking. 'Each and every one of them has reason to hate Gustavo Veloso. Each and every one is a good, God-fearing human being...but...' He paused again and Ria felt his hand tighten on her arm. 'If I were to tell them you were the woman of Veloso, the new untarnished bride he'd waited six years to enjoy, and invited them to take their pleasure with you first... I doubt if many of them would remember they were loving family men. They'd only recall they were men who'd been humbled and abused...but still men for all that...and they wouldn't need a second invitation.'

'You wouldn't.' Ria hardly breathed the denial, knowing instinctively there were few things the man at her side would not do.

'I wouldn't want to.' The firm reply held no reassurance. 'Neither would I want to shear off your beautiful hair and roll you naked in the mud before delivering you on his doorstep...' He paused to watch the empty horror masking her face. 'But equally I should regret even more the sight of Veloso flaunting his virgin prize as the sign of God's reward of his munificence!'

From somewhere Ria dredged up enough strength to oppose the tall menacing figure of her host. 'So you offer me two choices—rape by the masses—or rape by you.' There was a wealth of scorn in her bitter voice. 'What makes you think I would prefer the latter to the former? The labourers might be misguided—but you...' Her eyes flashed a sapphire fire. '*You*, Vitor Fortunato, are evil personified!'

She had expected a violent reaction and had steeled herself for it. Instead she received a slight formal bow.

'I regret it appears I failed to make my proposal absolutely clear. My purpose in offering you marriage is to prevent Gustavo Veloso from making you his wife... and, incidentally, your life a misery. It is not my intention to exercise the usual rights of a husband in the bedroom.'

Then as Ria stared at him at a complete loss for words, unsure whether she understood him or not, he left her in no possible doubt.

'Your virginity will remain as safe in my custody as it has for the past six years of your religious retreat.'

CHAPTER THREE

THE sound of approaching footsteps saved Ria from making any retort.

'Ah, food.' Vitor Fortunato moved towards the door as it opened to admit Floriana, a laden tray in her hands. 'Simple fare but sustaining, and I doubt if you are used to much better.'

He pulled out a plain table from against the wall, and taking the tray from the woman placed it down with a word of thanks, as with a quick glance at Ria she left the room, closing the door quietly behind her.

Could she expect help from that quarter? Ria doubted it. The look in the *mestizo*'s eyes had been one of mute adoration as she had gazed at the tall man who had relieved her of her burden.

At least, she thought, as the spicy smell of the *feijoada* assailed her nostrils, she wasn't being starved into submission—but then there was no need for that, was there? Not with the unspeakable fate with which she had been threatened!

'Here.' Her captor indicated she resumed her seat as he proffered her a small tray on which sat a plate amply filled with a mixture of black beans and meat over a base of rice. 'You'll feel better after you've eaten.'

Ria would have liked to refuse the meal, but in truth her body was crying out for sustenance and she knew she would need every ounce of her strength if she were to escape from this situation. Meekly she obeyed him, adding a small helping of shredded kale to her plate and accepting his offer of pepper and lemon sauce.

30

She watched Vitor covertly as he filled his own plate and came to sit opposite her once more, balancing another tray across his firm thighs. What was he, this man? Some fanatic, obviously, with a vested hatred against her guardian, determined to pursue a personal vendetta.

Solemnly she tasted her food and found it good. While her mouth was full the opportunity for speech was limited but there was nothing to prevent her brain from working.

She would make one last plea to be released and if that failed she would have to attempt to leave without his permission or knowledge! They had travelled across country, but only to avoid detection. She was sure there must be a road nearby. If only she could get out of the house and find it, eventually it must lead to a main road and hopefully from there she would be able to hitch a lift back to Campinas.

Fortunately she remembered the address because all the letters she had written over the years had been addressed to it, never to the main residence her guardian had in São Paolo. For a moment her thoughts dwelt on that fact. It was strange Veloso had insisted she only ever wrote to him at his country retreat. She had assumed it was to keep her letters separate from his business correspondence, but now, with Vitor's allegations fresh in her mind, the first thread of doubt was spun, only to be hastily banished as she accepted the long fruit drink he handed to her as he removed the tray with its now empty plate.

'Senhor Fortunato.' She addressed him pleadingly, the slight break in her voice adding pathos to her words. 'If you would let me go now, send one of your men with me to guide me to the main road, I promise not to mention your name to my guardian when I reach him.'

She observed with unease a slight smile lingering on his hard curved mouth as she took a sip of her drink, hoping to ease the soreness of her parched throat, guessing nerves as much as the well seasoned food to be its cause.

The liquid was cool and refreshingly tangy—slightly different from anything she had ever tasted before. But then Brazil grew a multitude of fruit and the convent kitchen had never been self-indulgent.

As she watched his enigmatic expression over the rim of her glass, instinct told her his mind was made up and she had little chance of changing it, but still she had to persevere. If she found herself unable to escape, the alternatives he had promised her were too dreadful to contemplate.

Ria licked the sweetness lingering on her lips as the man opposite her poured himself a drink from the same jug, sitting down again, stretching out his long legs and regarding her with a sombre interest as she tried to find an argument to move him.

'Can't you see,' she burst out, leaning forward and pinioning his gaze with steady blue eyes. 'You'll never get away with this crazy idea! Even now my guardian will be searching for me. I imagine the car has already been discovered. It can only be a matter of time before the police arrive.'

'I doubt it, Ria.' He shook his dark head. 'And since we are shortly to become man and wife it's ridiculous for you to be so formal. You know my Christian name— use it.'

Damn his patronising arrogance! Blue fire blazed from Ria's lovely eyes.

'You claim to be a Christian?' The condemnation had sprung to her tongue despite all her good intentions to keep calm, she was too incensed by his intractability to

restrain her temper. 'Then why don't you act like one—
or have you forgotten the Lord claimed vengeance for
himself?' She heaved in a deep breath. 'Whatever
grievance you imagine you have against Senhor Veloso,
you have no right to extort payment—and particularly
not by using an innocent person as a tool!'

'Ah, but it is your innocence that makes you the
perfect tool, *meu amor*,' he rejoined mockingly. 'It's the
one thing Veloso craves for himself above all other and
therefore the one thing I mean to deny him by whatever
means I have.'

His dark eyes passed with thoughtful appraisal over
her tense body, gravely admiring. 'I wish you no harm.
In fact the prospect of rescuing you from such a lib-
ertine adds a further attraction to the plan I have
devised.'

'But you've no rights over my destiny whatsoever!'
Infuriated by his calmness, Ria took a long draught of
her drink as she tried to stop her feelings getting out of
control. 'And your claim to have my interests at heart
is a monstrous lie, since you threaten to offer me as a
plaything to your beastly confederates!'

'The choice is yours,' came the cool response. 'You
speak only of the less attractive option. As my wife you
will have respect and honour. You will be well fed and
suitably clothed . . . and you won't be prevailed upon to
perform any acts you find offensive or demeaning. What
more could a girl who started life in the *favelas* of São
Paolo want? If it's Veloso's wealth that attracts you,
then you will be paying a heavy price to live in its
shadow!'

'Gustavo Veloso is a good man, a generous man!' Ria
was on her feet, her fingers gripping the sides of her
glass as if she would crush it. 'He befriended me, and
now when I can repay some of his kindness I mean to
do just that! I don't believe any of your filthy lies. All

he wants to be to me is a father—not a husband. And I mean to give him that opportunity.' Her chin came up proudly as Vitor rose slowly to his feet with a controlled dangerous power. 'You may consider I spoke only of the less attractive alternative—to my mind it's the better! Anything rather then bear the name of a madman! The only way you'll prevent me from returning to my guardian is by killing me!'

'I am no murderer!' Hard hands grasped her shoulders. 'But you're a fool if you believe Veloso will welcome you if your purity is lost.' He gave a brutal laugh. 'He has too many second-hand women at his call already, wanton and willing, prepared to cater to his depraved appetite. What would he want with a white body like yours which shrinks at a man's touch and trembles to be held in a man's arms? Eh, *meu amor*? Unless it was an unplayed instrument which he could tune to his own scale?'

'You're disgusting.' Ria suppressed a sob. She was shaking in his grasp, and little wonder, since his hands bound her so tightly. So what if she was wary of men? Hadn't she enough cause? She could still remember the drunken brawls and the wife-beatings that had been a nightly occurrence in the poor, broken-down hovels where she had spent her early life.

'I'm realistic, Ria,' he insisted quietly. His face was so close to hers that she could feel his warm breath on her cheek, smell the clean, tangy aroma of his skin. A strange unsettling glissando of sensation trembled through her, beginning where his warm hands imprisoned her, spreading through her body in an unknown frightening surge.

'Dear God, *menina*! Even if I were to change my plans it would be too late for your safety. The whole set-up was planned to look like a ritual abduction—a planned

elopement. Do you think your so-called guardian would
forgive you that?'

Now she realised the meaning and importance of that
humiliating kiss! Ria's hand rose to her mouth remem-
bering the sensation of his hungry mouth against her
own. If such an elopement had been genuine it would
mean her guardian would lose face, first because she
had carried on a liaison unknown to him, and secondly
because in the eyes of his countrymen he would be less
of a man because he had been unable to protect her from
the results of her own weaknesses.

But he cared for her! She had to believe that. Resolutely she forced the memory of his heavy-jowled face
and coldly assessing eyes from her mind. It wasn't
necessary for a man to be physically attractive to be a
humanitarian. The inexplicable antipathy she had felt
towards his gross presence on the few occasions when
he had visited her had surely been a sign of her own
immaturity? Of course he would believe her story—
accept her in his home in the role of his daughter as he
had always intended, heal and avenge the wounds inflicted on her.

'He would! He would!' She shouted the words in her
anguish. 'He's a philanthropist!'

Abruptly her arms were released as Vitor strode with
quick strides to the door, opening it to bellow out a name,
'Manuel!'

What now, Ria thought in agitation, tossing the re-
mainder of her drink down her throat before replacing
the glass safely on the table, her breath catching suddenly as her heart missed a beat. Had the impassioned
brigand who had captured her grown tired of talking?
Was he about to put his threat into action?

Like a wounded animal she cowered back against the
wall, her fingers clutching the folds of her dress as Vitor

turned from the door, a large heavy man immediately behind him.

'No.' It was little more than a whimper as her bravery drained away in the face of such an overpowering threat. The newcomer was like a giant, heavy, bearded, his face oddly vacant as his broad mouth broke into a simpering smile.

'Pretty,' he murmured, bright eyes more childlike than adult. 'Pretty, pretty lady.'

He took two shambling steps towards her, stopping with the smile freezing on his face as she uttered a gasping shriek.

'Don't be afraid, Ria.' It was Vitor Fortunato's voice, deep and steady, which broke through her terror. 'Manuel won't hurt you. He was a man with much machismo before he became as he is. Even now his gentleness remains when most of his intelligence has gone.'

'I don't understand.' Ria pushed the weight of her hair away from her damp neck, fearful less she should faint and place herself totally at the mercy of these alien creatures.

'Show her your arm, Manuel.' It was a careful command softly voiced as Ria allowed her eyes to travel to where Vitor had flung a careless arm round the giant's shoulders.

'Oh!' Her exclamation of mingled shock and pity as she saw for the first time that an empty sleeve hung where Manuel's right arm should have been rent the simmering tension. As he moved to unpin it Ria felt the ground beneath her begin to heave and a welcome darkness come to receive her.

Her faint must have lasted only seconds but when she regained consciousness she was alone in the room with

Vitor, his hand pressed down on her neck, forcing her head between her knees.

'I'm all right now.' She felt his hand removed and flung herself back thankfully in the chair, closing her eyes, trying to regain her strength.

'I won't apologise for that,' Vitor was saying from somewhere quite near at hand. 'It was the best way I could demonstrate the type of man Veloso is. His money has come from the poor lands of the north-east where he owns great tracts of property which are exploited at the expense of the men who work them on his behalf.'

'Manuel lost his arm in a cane-cutting machine, badly serviced, without the safety guards that should have been in place. He was working late and fast because his children were starving and he needed more money, and...' he paused graphically. 'You saw with your own eyes what happened. He bled so much before he was discovered that he went into a coma and was left not only disabled but brain-damaged. That's the kind of man your philanthropist is. Manuel didn't receive even one *cruzado* in compensation.'

'An accident.' Ria's eyelids fluttered open. 'Anyone can have an accident. It wasn't Senhor Veloso's fault. I won't believe the wicked things you are saying about him. I won't!'

Tears more of frustration and rage than fear trickled down her pale cheeks.

'You stubborn little fool!' Irritation coloured Vitor's tone. 'It seems the drink has befuddled your senses. Perhaps after a good night's rest you will see things more clearly.'

'Drink?' Doubtful blue eyes searched for the empty glass she had discarded. 'You mean the fruit juice?'

Vitor nodded. 'With a lacing of *cachaca*. Haven't you ever heard of a *batida*?'

Ria shot him a vengeful look. Of course she had heard of the drink made from fruit juice and the strong white rum of Brazil. The trouble was she had never tasted one. She raised her hand to brush her newly burning cheeks. Dear heavens, would there be no end to the dreadful experiences of this day?

Vitor's gentle laughter did nothing to relieve her discomfort.

'I'll get Floriana to show you to your room. Sleep would seem to be your most desired friend, but should you need anything in the night I shall be near by. Just give me a call, you know my name.' The chiselled mouth tossed her a nonchalant grin. 'Vitor.'

'Thank you, Senhor Fortunato.' Ria loaded his hated name with a deep sarcasm. 'But nothing you've said or shown me has made any difference to the way I feel. Do with me as you will. I will agree to nothing, neither shall I ask anything from you—not even mercy!'

Alone in the stark little bedroom with its simple whitewashed walls, Ria's hands closed convulsively round the robe of unbleached cotton she had been given to wear for a nightgown.

Her eyes surveyed the room from beneath the golden bar of her furrowed eyebrows. The window through which the warm scented air drifted was large but barred. There was no escape that way.

On the other hand the door, though heavily built, had no lock in it and she hadn't heard any bolt drawn across it from the outside. Could she simply walk out that way if she was careful?

Vitor Fortunato thought she was exhausted, her tiredness accentuated by alcohol—probably administered deliberately for that very purpose, she thought grimly. And she *was* tired. Bone-achingly so. But if he thought she would be so easily discouraged he was mistaken! She was made of sterner stuff than he had anticipated.

A penniless waif from the streets. Yes, she couldn't argue with that description, but she'd been bred with spirit and endurance in her bones—her mother the beautiful only child of a rich Brazilian industrialist who had given her heart and body to the man she loved, only to be disowned and thrown out of her family home by the father who had claimed to adore her when she'd confessed to her unwed pregnancy and begged his clemency; her father, the clever brave Englishman whose looks she had inherited, and whose stay in Brazil had been a short respite from a dangerous secret job he hadn't been at liberty to disclose—even to the woman he'd loved and sworn to marry when his duty was discharged. Only, of course, there had been no fairytale ending. Although her mother had never given up hope of hearing again from her lover, the passing years had brought nothing but silence.

A shudder of disgust ran through Ria's nerves as her mind lingered on the role her maternal grandfather had played in events. In the first instance he had resolutely refused Caterina's pleas to be allowed to marry the Englishman with whom she had fallen so desperately in love. Caterina, herself, had never tried to excuse herself for the sin of anticipating the marriage which was destined never to be, had accepted her banishment with dignity when it was clear her father would never relent, but later had sunk her pride one last time to implore his help on behalf of her young daughter. He had walked from the room, leaving her to be shown out of the house by a servant, his face set like stone. They had been Caterina's own words when, too distraught for discretion, she had allowed Ria to see the extent of her misery.

Ria heaved a deep sigh. How often she had wondered whether, had her grandfather's wife been alive, she would have softened the heart of the arrogant patriarch, whose name Caterina had vowed never to utter again after the last painful rebuff. But her grandmother had died when her only child had been scarcely a few hours old.

What about her own father, she wondered? All she knew about the man who had sired her was what her mother had told her, and the faded photograph of the two of them which had been one of her most treasured belongings, safeguarded in the small Bible she had kept in her possession throughout the traumas of her childhood. Now even that was lost to her.

Caught in a downward spiral of misery, Ria admitted to herself that nothing had been more traumatic than the moment she had realised her mother was dead—her love and support lost to her forever. How could she ever forget the abject terror she had felt as she had run sobbing down the unlit, muddy tracks between the makeshift structures that served as homes for the hundreds of São Paolo's destitute inhabitants, to arrive dirty and distraught outside Aunt Luisa's small room.

Dear Aunt Luisa, she thought now, with a spasm of sorrow that she had lost touch with her mother's truest friend. Not only had the older woman arranged for Caterina to have a decent burial, but if it hadn't been for her compassion in befriending Ria herself, she would have had no option but to join the other children as unfortunate as herself—living off scraps, sleeping by the warm-air grids from the subways, evading the police patrols on their routine raids where they rounded up the young vagrants.

How easily she could have spent her teens in Febeng, the Government-sponsored institute for destitute children instead of in the welcoming, if slightly austere, cloisters of St Augustine's convent. For if Luisa hadn't taken her in, Veloso would never have been able to make his offer.

Yes, she acknowledged wearily, the last few years of her life had indeed been privileged, but they hadn't completely eliminated the strong instinct for survival that the earlier times of hardship had generated!

Forcing herself to keep awake, Ria sat uncomfortably on the edge of the bed waiting for darkness and silence.

It was past midnight when she dared to open the door and steal out into the passageway which led to the main living-room and beyond that to the only door the farmhouse boasted.

The living-room was in darkness, but the door stood open as soundlessly she crossed the threshold, moving slowly forward trying to recall the layout of the room as she had last seen it.

'Go back to bed, Ria. You'll never find your way to the road in the dark without guidance, and I shall have the inconvenience of riding out to find you to bring you back in the morning, when I'd far rather be enjoying my breakfast.'

Ria started so violently at the sound of Vitor's calm voice that she moved forward without thinking, collided with the sharp edge of the table, and uttered a sharp cry of pain.

'Damn you, Vitor Fortunato!' she blazed, throwing caution to the winds as deep disappointment welled up inside her, and she turned in the direction of his voice.

'For certain I am damned already, so your curses leave me unmoved, Maria Bernardi.'

As a dim light filled the room she could see him sprawled out in an armchair, his eyes broody with sleep, his jaw dark with beard. He appeared totally relaxed, but it was the relaxation of a jungle cat, Ria sensed. Any sharp movement on her part and he would spring at her with as little mercy as the lean lithe jaguar that stalked the Amazon valley.

'I was looking for the bathroom,' she lied with a haughty movement of her head. Vitor looked capable of anything and she wasn't going to invite his retribution. Every hour she could keep away from harm was another sixty minutes of grace to enable either the police or her guardian to find her.

'You were trying to run away.' He pulled himself to his feet as Ria stood her ground, her hand rising to her breast in an abortive attempt to calm the wild racing of her heart at his approach. 'I'm a light sleeper, Ria,' he continued mildly. 'And even if I weren't, the dogs would wake me as soon as you stepped outside the door.'

'Dogs?' Her face flushed in mortification. They were a hazard she hadn't contemplated.

'Another phobia?' he asked drily. 'To add to the existing ones of men and horses?'

'I'm not afraid of horses!' His mocking smile forced her into contradiction. 'It's just that I'd never ridden before. And I like dogs too,' she declared strongly. After all she was no shrinking violet to be protected from domestic beasts. 'But only a fool would pat a guard dog.'

'Precisely.' He moved towards her. 'So that leaves men.' He reached out a hand as she moved instinctively away from his grasp. She was certainly frightened of his threats, but somehow she sensed a warmth about Vitor that was totally foreign to what he had proposed. She acknowledged to herself that she was wary of him, but she wasn't terrified. And that was strange because in the position she was in, she should have been.

'Don't touch me!' she snapped angrily.

He stopped instantly, allowing his hand to fall to his side.

'You hurt your leg on the table. Does it need attention?'

'No. No, thank you.' She rejected his offer brusquely as her hand moved to touch the sore front of her thigh. There would be a bruise there tomorrow, but why should she care? Unless she could persuade the man who regarded her so intently to relent, it would be only one of many.

She was pressed back as far as she could retreat now, so when he touched her cheek with a lazy finger she could do nothing but grit her teeth and endure his touch. He was very close to her. So close that every nerve in her body was responding to his presence—his body warmth, the sharp clean scent of his skin. His nearness was overpowering as he loomed over her.

'Poor Ria,' he intoned ruefully. 'Your eyes look as bruised from lack of sleep as your bones must be from your journey here.'

Amazed by the throb of compassion in his voice, the soft pity in the dark eyes that dwelt on her face, Ria grasped his hand with trembling fingers.

'Vitor,' she begged urgently, using his name for the first time. 'Can't you see no good can come of this? Please, please set me free.' She was near to weeping but pride held her tears in check as he stared down at her.

He shook his dark head slowly. 'Even if I did, it would be too late for you. You would have spent the night under another man's roof. If Veloso did take you in, he'd make your life hell.'

'Then let that be your vengeance,' she responded eagerly, pushing to the back of her mind the memory of how her own mother had been so cruelly rejected for breaking the strict Brazilian code of morals. 'I'll take my chance with him.'

'Hm.' Vitor emitted a brief humourless laugh. 'You're a lot braver and more stubborn than I'd expected. Go back to bed—tomorrow I may be able to change your mind.'

There was only one way she could take that remark. The blood drained from her face as she gave a strangled gasp of horror. Vitor's brow darkened angrily as she felt her body shudder and begin to fall.

'Dear God!' There was a bitter fury in his voice as he swept her up into his arms before she hit the floor. 'Do you really imagine the men here so much lack honour that they'd treat you with anything less than total respect?' Her eyes were closed, but she heard his words plainly as his arms tightened around her. 'And do you really imagine I would allow anyone to harm as much as a single hair on your beautiful golden head?'

Ria felt too emotionally exhausted to answer as she found an unexpected pleasure in being held so close to the steady beat of Vitor's heart. She was only aware that she was being carried back to her room and laid gently down on her bed.

'Sleep now, *menina*. There is still one way left to persuade you to my way of thinking.'

Something touched her temple and for a wild moment she imagined it had been the soft velvet touch of Vitor's lips. But when she looked up he was moving away from her.

The door closed gently behind him as, unable to fight her body's aching need for rest, Ria commended her soul to God, shut her eyes and slept.

CHAPTER FOUR

A HEAVY series of knocks on her door brought Ria back to her senses. Swinging her legs off the bed and wincing at their unaccustomed stiffness, she hastily tried to straighten her crumpled dress before going to open it.

Outside Vitor stood, his eyes shuttered through lack of sleep, his chin swarthy with dark beard.

As memories of the previous evening flooded back to her, Ria raised her hand to her hair, trying to brush its chaotic tumble away from her face. Somehow she hadn't expected Vitor to pay her the courtesy of knocking when he could so easily have walked in. Despite the assurances of the previous night she was still his prisoner, wasn't she?

'Forgive me for waking you so abruptly.' He gave her an odd little bow accompanied by a twist of his firm mouth that could have been a smile. 'But it's nearly ten o'clock and there's a visitor here to see you.'

A policeman? Senhor Veloso himself or one of his colleagues? There was no way Ria could hide her delight as she pushed past Vitor and entered the main living-room.

The woman who rose to greet her was in her fifties. Once in her youth she might have been beautiful, but now her high-boned face was lined, the skin rough. Hair that had once been black as a raven's wing was heavily streaked with grey, coarse and lifeless. Only the eyes, large and lustrous, still showed anything of what she might have been as a young girl.

Ria had been a child of thirteen when she had last seen that beloved face and in her wildest dreams she had never thought to set eyes on it again. Unbelievably, she had received a miraculous answer to her desperate prayers!

'Aunt Luisa! Oh, Aunt Luisa!' Ria's voice broke as tears ran uncontrollably down her cheeks. 'It really is you, isn't it—or am I going mad?'

'Ria—my dearest Ria.' Luisa Ferreira rose to her feet, moving with a grace that belied a body plump from malnutrition rather than greed. 'Yes, it's truly me. Oh, my dear girl, how beautiful you've grown! How very proud Caterina would have been to see you now.' She hugged Ria closely to her, her hands moving convulsively against the young girl's shoulders. 'Dear God, forgive me for what I've done!'

The last dramatic cry wrung pity as well as amazement from Ria as the older woman released her hold on her and stood away to gaze at her with pain-stricken eyes.

A lance of disquiet pierced Ria's heart. Was Luisa not, after all, the ally she had supposed her? A feeling of coldness flooded through her limbs, as reason overtook emotion. How could she be a friend when Vitor had given her such ready access to his fortress? She had been betrayed. The joy of the reunion was instantly neutralised by the ugly suspicion of Luisa's perfidy.

'What have you done?' The question was a mere breath on Ria's dry lips.

'I let him take you.' The uncompromising reply was equally soft as Luisa turned her head away as if unable to meet the younger woman's gaze.

For a moment Ria let her glance linger where Vitor stood motionless against the doorpost, a silent audience to the confrontation before him.

'You mean you still work for my guardian—that you knew of my travel arrangements—and you told him?' Her head jerked in Vitor's direction. 'So that he could abduct me?'

Luisa nodded. 'Yes,' she agreed simply. 'All that is true, but it wasn't what I meant. My crime was allowing Gustavo Veloso to take you away from me, to assume authority over you.' Her face contorted with bitter emotion as she paused, as if struggling to find the right words before continuing in a voice racked with pain. 'As God is my judge, Ria, I truly believed him when he swore all he wanted to do was make amends for what he had done to your mother. Not that I cared one iota for the salvation of his immortal soul, but he deserved to pay for the misery he inflicted on Caterina, and who was I to stand in your way of enjoying a rich and fruitful future?' She shook her head as if unable to credit her own stupidity. 'It was because I loved you and wanted the best for you that I allowed myself to believe Veloso had your best interests at heart.' Her voice broke.

Her mind reeling from what she had heard, totally unable to make any sense of it, Ria's first action was to fling her arms in a loving gesture round the other woman. 'I know you loved me,' she assured her gently. 'I'm sure you tried to do your best for me, but I don't understand what this is all about! Why are you here? What have you got to do with—with him?' Once more she indicated the silent form of Vitor Fortunato by a gesture of her flaxen head. 'And what has my mother got to do with it?' Her troubled eyes pleaded for an explanation.

'Tell her, Luisa.' The voice from the watching man was deep, unemotional, his face expressionless. 'Tell Ria what you told me, how you first came to know her mother, and what happened.'

'It was ten or so years ago.' Luisa obeyed him, turning away from Ria momentarily to sink down on a chair. Without a word Ria, too, seated herself opposite the older woman, waiting for her to speak again. She didn't have long to wonder as with a sigh Luisa picked up the thread of her story.

'Caterina was employed in the Veloso household in São Paolo as a personal maid to Senhora Veloso. You must have been about eight at the time, but your mother kept your existence a secret from everyone because the Senhora was very proper, very moral. If she'd found out Caterina was an unmarried mother she would have lost her job, and after the lean years she had already suffered she couldn't risk dismissal.' She stopped her narrative to sigh deeply.

'After a short time she and I became friends and she eventually confided in me; that's when I first met you.' She smiled faintly as Ria nodded, having searched her memory and found a hazy recollection of first seeing Luisa in one of the city parks.

Leaning forward, her soulful eyes fixed on Ria's innocent blue eyes, she went on. 'Then one day Veloso himself saw Caterina out in the street with you and became suspicious. He made enquiries and found out that you were her child and had been conceived and born out of wedlock.'

'He sacked her?' It was the obvious answer, and Ria felt sick imagining what her mother had felt.

'He did worse than that,' Luisa informed her bitterly. 'He made her a proposition. Either she became his unofficial mistress or he denounced her publicly as a harlot with an illegitimate child and ensured she never got another job in a respectable household.'

'I—I can't believe it!' Ria faltered. But she was beginning to. There was a deep sincerity on the older woman's face that defied doubt. 'Go on,' she encouraged her quietly, knowing she must hear her out however agonising the ordeal.

Black-covered shoulders shrugged. 'Naturally Caterina turned him down. He became violent, beating her up and throwing her out into the street—quite literally. He threatened her that if she told anyone what had happened between them he would accuse her of trying to steal his wife's emeralds.'

At the back of Ria's mind a memory stirred. Her mother coming home hardly able to walk, her face bruised and bleeding. The nine-year-old child had rushed towards her crying for her mother's pain, wanting to help, not knowing what to do.

Caterina Bernardi had cuddled her stricken daughter, calming her down, telling her she had fallen down the stairs at 'the big house' where she worked, but it was all right. Aunt Luisa was here to help her. She had brought her home and was going to bathe her face, and it would never happen again because she was never going back to that place.

Appalled, Ria looked from Luisa to Vitor who hadn't moved a muscle during the recital. 'I remember that.' Her mouth was so dry the words stuck in her throat. 'But I never realised she worked in Gustavo Veloso's house.'

But then, of course, Caterina wouldn't have told her, wouldn't have wanted her young daughter to let the knowledge slip out when it was so important her existence was kept secret. All she had known was that her mother worked at 'the big house'. And after she left there, there had followed four years of poverty and misery ending in disaster.

'It's all true,' Vitor confirmed, an edge of compassion softening the clear-cut tone of his deep voice. 'Like everything else I've told you.'

'But—but . . .' Ria stammered unhappily. 'If he was so wicked to my mother why did you agree . . .' Her voice trailed away, but her shocked eyes desperately sought an explanation from Luisa.

'It wasn't an easy decision.' The older woman swallowed with difficulty. 'I would willingly have shared what little I had with you, but it was so very, very little. I'll never forget the day he called me up from below stairs and told me he knew you were living with me since Caterina's death. He swore his repentance, begged me to let him repay to the daughter what he could never repay to the mother.' She made an angry gesture with her hands. 'I had my doubts, of course I did! You were thirteen and already showing the promise of becoming the beautiful young woman you are today, but he was very persuasive, and I allowed myself to agree to what he suggested. I even believed him when he said no one was to know what he was doing, not even his wife, because he didn't want publicity. He didn't want credit for righting a terrible wrong.'

'It was a good education.' Her mind spinning, it was all Ria could think of to say. 'Couldn't it have been an act of contrition?'

'Huh!' Luisa's exclamation was harsh. 'It was an act of selfishness and lust. He had one idea in mind from the beginning. He hadn't been able to seduce Caterina so instead he would have Caterina's daughter. She'd have no means of eluding him, because he would keep her safe in a convent until the time was right for him to make her his wife. You see, he already knew his present wife was mortally ill.'

'No, oh, no!' It was a strangled gasp from Ria as for the first time she found herself accepting what Vitor had already told her and fighting the idea with every last shred of her courage.

Luisa regarded her ashen face with great pity. 'The whole household at Campinas—where I'm now working—knows that now Veloso is a widower he is bringing back his new bride-to-be from Salvador and plans an immediate wedding.' There was a wealth of pain in the older woman's careworn face as she continued relentlessly. 'I was distraught with anger and anxiety as soon as I heard what was happening. I knew I had to do something to get you out of his grasp. It was then I remembered Senhor Fortunato.' She cast a fleeting smile at the dark figure by the door. 'Not only was there no love lost between him and Senhor Veloso—that was common knowledge—but Senhor Fortunato was a clever and educated man. I thought, prayed, that he might be able to invoke the law to thwart Veloso's obscene intentions.' Her countenance was transformed by the brilliance of her smile. 'He promised he would move heaven and earth—to rescue you.'

'I have a great respect for the law,' Vitor interposed quietly. 'But sometimes there are other, more satisfying solutions to a problem.'

'You can trust him, Ria my love.' Luisa's eyes brimmed with tears. 'I'm prepared to stake my life on that.'

In doubt no longer, Ria could picture her mother's anguished face in her mind's eye, recalling the proud beautiful lines that had mirrored an indomitable spirit. Caterina hadn't sacrificed so much for her only daughter to fall a prey to the monster who had ruined her one last hope of a healthy, happy life!

'I won't marry him. I won't!' Panic streamed through her harsh rejection. 'I'd do anything rather than that!'

'Anything?'

The cool query came from the lounging figure in the doorway as Vitor lifted a lazy eyebrow.

Raising her wide-eyed gaze to his dark saturnine visage Ria felt the painful thunder of her heart. She was stunned by what she had just heard. Too stunned to argue the matter further with him. By producing Luisa he had beaten her and he knew it. To go to Veloso in any capacity would be to betray her mother. Even the money he had invested in her education seemed unimportant. Yes, she would do anything to escape the fate planned for her. But she had little to offer a depressed job-market. Even her skills as a housekeeper and companion would stand her in poor stead. She was young, without experience and, she admitted without vanity, too outstandingly different in appearance from the dark Brazilian girls to be welcomed in their households by the passionate, jealous Brazilian senhoras.

Alone and unprotected, without money, she would have no hiding place from Gustavo Veloso's anger at her defection. Now she had been shown the true nature of her guardian's character, she suppressed a cold shiver of fear, her fertile imagination paintng a graphic picture of how he would react when he found her...and find her he undoubtedly would!

'Well, Ria?' Vitor prompted gently as she made no move to answer his question.

She had no real choice open to her if she wanted to preserve both her skin and her mother's honour. It wasn't as if Vitor intended to consummate their proposed marriage. As his nominal wife she would have both his protection and that of the law. So ran her tumultuous thoughts before she gave him the answer he so patiently awaited.

'Yes,' she told him, her tone carefully controlled. 'Anything.'

She was only dimly aware of Luisa Ferreira rising and coming towards her, murmuring something about returning to Campinas before her absence was remarked on, and kissing her gently on both cheeks. 'He even told me it was in your best interests to make a complete break with the past. It was he who arranged for you to be told I'd moved away.' The older woman's mouth twisted wryly. 'There was no way I could communicate with you myself, and it was too dangerous to ask anyone for help. Besides,' she shuddered with distaste, 'I still thought at the time he had your best interests at heart, as he'd said.'

'Don't worry, Aunt Luisa.' Ria forced herself to smile as she clasped the other woman's hand with loving fervour. 'You've nothing to blame yourself for, nothing.'

She had no idea how much time passed before Vitor was standing before her thrusting a tray of coffee and warm rolls into her hands.

'Eat, *menina*,' he instructed kindly. 'I'm a man who likes his women to be curvaceous.' The tone was humorous but the eyes that regarded her closely were cool and questioning, as if he half expected her to change her mind.

'Thank you.' She gave him a tremulous smile. 'I don't know what shocked me more—meeting Aunt Luisa again or listening to what she had to say.' She picked up a roll, the tenseness of her fingers causing it to crumble. 'One thing puzzled me, Vitor.'

'Ask it.' His tolerant smile invited her confidence.

'You obviously knew I'd trust her. Why didn't you arrange for her to come here straight away instead of making all those other dreadful threats?' Blue eyes accused him bravely.

'Because I underestimated your strength of purpose and courage,' he told her simply. 'And I overestimated, too, my own powers of persuasion.' He gave her a long stare. 'At times I went too far in my enthusiasm to ensure your co-operation, but I react badly to being thwarted.'

'I find it difficult to determine whether it's pride or shame that colours that confession,' Ria retorted a little tartly. His powers of persuasion were undoubtedly a force to be reckoned with, she admitted silently to herself. 'But that's not an answer to my question.'

'Fear.' The terse reply was instant this time. 'To put it bluntly, Luisa is terrified in case Veloso associates her with present events. He's no fool and will realise someone has given away private information. She won't be the only person to come under suspicion, but if she were seen to be leaving the house and making for an unknown destination...' He paused meaningfully. 'When she first came to me she begged I should do everything without implicating her, unless there was no other alternatives.

'Oh!' Ria gulped miserably. 'Then I've put her in danger.'

Vitor gave a short humourless laugh. 'Life is full of risks, and no one is more aware of that than Luisa. She came here willingly enough when she learned of the stand you'd taken. I can assure you I've taken every possible precaution to see that no one discovers where and with whom she has been, and I have friends who will continue to guard her interests, I promise you.' The look he gave her was long and lingering. 'And as for you, Maria Bernardi...'

'Yes?' She was no longer afraid of the proud man who held her future in his strong capable hands, as an unexpected calmness filled her inner being.

'I have arranged for the local priest, who is a good friend of mine, to be here in an hour. After that, *meu amor*, you'll belong to me and no one can lay claim to you or hurt you!'

*   *   *

It was in fact just over an hour later that Maria Bernardi and Vitor Fortunato became man and wife in a short service conducted in the plantation chapel with a handful of the workers present as witnesses.

Vitor was darkly impressive as the groom, freshly shaven, immaculate in light trousers and a loose toning jacket. Stealing a glance at his bold profile as they stood before the small altar, Ria felt her heart leap.

He was a handsome man, this impressive, dangerous stranger into whose hands she had given her life. Standing beside him newly bathed, her hair gleaming like a veil of gold on her slim shoulders, Ria regretted she wasn't wearing something more attractive.

However meaningless the ceremony in the true sense, since they didn't love each other or intend to live together truly as man and wife, it was still a sacrament and binding. It would have been nice to have worn something pretty instead of the same old pale blue cotton dress. Newly steamed and pressed, it was true, but still the ugly garment in which she had been abducted.

She made her responses firmly, and after the ceremony when Vitor took her in his arms and kissed her gently on the lips she made no effort to draw away from him. Later, when to the delighted shouts from the small group of onlookers he had picked her up in his arms and run with her back into the farmhouse, kicking the door to behind them, she enjoyed the most marvellous feeling of warmth and security she had ever known since her mother's death.

Her new husband felt so good, so powerful and protective. He smelt so good too, she acknowledged delightedly, savouring the tangy scent of his skin, so unlike the mingled odours of sweat and incense that had always hovered around the convent priest. When he released her, bending to stand her upright in front of him, she actually felt a pang of regret.

'Poor Ria.' His white teeth gleamed as he tossed her a grin. 'You should have a big celebration, plenty of food and drink and a samba band playing for you on your wedding-day. As it is our friends believe we are too enamoured of each other to waste a second of our honeymoon, and therefore they will forgive us when we leave them so abruptly.'

'We're going somewhere?' She had not had time to think ahead.

'To São Paolo,' he nodded. 'I need a little time, but the sooner you are publicly acknowledged as my legal wife the safer you will be.' He touched her cheek with his hand, an affectionate gesture that brought the colour racing to her face. 'Veloso has no legal claim to you at all. He simply took you when there was no one to stop him, but I don't trust him not to go after you and do some mischief. In any case, we can't stay here. It can only be a matter of hours now before Veloso's men arrive to make enquiries and we mustn't be discovered. I can't compromise the farm manager and his family.'

'You're not the manager then?' Ria had assumed his presence there and the way he had acted implied just that.

Vitor shook his head absently. 'The landlord, not the manager,' he told her laconically. 'I arranged for him and his family to be away for a couple of days while I accomplished what I intended. This place is remote enough to take some finding, and I gambled on our being safe here for a little while at least.'

Ria swallowed. Vitor was a landowner? Then presumably he was a wealthy man. The knowledge gave her food for thought, and she found his behaviour even more extraordinary.

'Where are we staying in São Paolo?' she asked at last.

'I have an apartment. Small, but adequate.' He gave her a long searching look, moving from her head to her toes, missing nothing. 'At least you will have the opportunity to dress as befits the wife of Vitor Fortunato. The shops of São Paolo are among the best and most fashionable in the world.'

As if she didn't know! Ria mused silently, recalling the times she had peered into their enormous brightly lit windows, seeing them as some fairyland for ever barred to her. Only now, apparently, they weren't. A spurt of excitement sizzled through her—a wild tumultuous surge of high spirits which had lain dormant in her body for so long, dampened first by deprivation and afterwards by application as she had schooled herself to obey the stern dictates of her tutors.

She was no longer poor little Maria Bernardi. She was the wife of Vitor Fortunato—whatever that implied. A small dimple made a delightful dent in her cheek as her beautifully shaped mouth, warm and generous, as unadorned as nature had intended, lifted at the corners.

Yes, she was Fortune's bride. With no idea what she had let herself in for or what the future held for her, she would enjoy the present while she could.

'I'm ready to leave when you are,' she told him meekly.

CHAPTER FIVE

IT WAS late afternoon when they reached the tall apartment block in São Paolo, Vitor having elected not to stop on the road for food in case they should be seen and identified. But the journey had passed without incident, Ria slaking both her thirst and appetite en route as she had enjoyed the packed meal Floriana had provided for them.

Vitor's apartment was on the fourth floor. Small it might be, Ria assessed, her discerning glance roving round the main sitting-room, but only by comparison with something larger! By her own standards it was palatial. In truth she had seen nothing like it before. She stared in admiration at its contemporary elegance, taking in the teak and stainless steel fittings, the beautiful wood-block floor, the teak three-piece suite with its stone-coloured upholstery and the curtains at the large picture window, where brightly coloured birds of paradise weaved and soared against a background of pale blue. Romantic and dramatic, they were surely a woman's choice rather than a man's?

Magnetically attracted to their brilliance, Ria moved across to touch the fabric reverently with her fingers. It was polished cotton, cool and crisp against her skin.

'You approve?' Vitor was standing surveying her actions with unconcealed interest.

Ria nodded. 'They're beautiful.'

Reluctantly she released the edge of the curtain. 'Did you have an interior decorator pick them for you?'

'Hardly.' He gave her a brief but knowing look. 'But you're right to think I didn't choose them, although,' a slight shrug, 'I like them well enough. I suspect only a woman would want to turn a prosaic sitting-room into an exotic aviary.'

The note of strain, almost pain in his voice grated on her ears. He had shared this place with a woman...a lover? Someone who had deserted him or...? Ria felt a wretched sense of foreboding pass over her, someone he had deserted in order to avenge himself for some real or imagined wrong? Whichever it was, it made her own position even more difficult.

She bit her lips contemplatively. Vitor had told her he didn't intend to exercise the usual rights of a husband in the bedroom. Without that assurance and despite the alternatives facing her she doubted whether she would have agreed to go through the wedding-service with him. Her face brightened as she saw a solution. The woman who had shared the apartment with him loved him so much she had agreed to his plan. She, Ria, would be his legal wife and the other woman would continue to be his mistress! It was the perfect answer, relieving her as it did of any obligations her vows would have placed her under should Vitor have changed his mind about sharing her bed!'

Turning to Vitor she gave him a glowing, unrestrained smile. 'What's her name?' Then in answer to his puzzled frown, 'The lady who chose the curtains?'

'Oh.' He paused for what seemed an interminable time. Surely he didn't think she would be jealous of his having another attachment? Just when she had given up hope of receiving an answer Vitor said simply, 'Marta. Her name's Marta.'

Acknowledging his reply with a quick nod of her head, filing the name for future reference, Ria changed the subject brightly.

'Could I see the kitchen now?'

'Of course.' Vitor opened a door leading off the main room. 'I'm looking forward to seeing proof that the money spent on you during the past six years was well invested,' he informed her drily.

'Oh!' Despite her previous resolutions Ria experienced a twinge of guilt. It couldn't have been cheap paying for her to be at the convent all those years. All through the holidays, too. Of course it didn't mean Veloso was entitled to force her into marriage with him, but she couldn't help feeling like a thief when she considered the expense involved.

'What is it, Ria? Does the prospect of catering for this aspect of my appetite affront you so badly? I promise you I'm not too hard a task-master.'

He had seen the worry sitting on her countenance like a dark cloud and responded to alleviate it. It was a casual enough question but there was nothing casual about the dark eyes that demanded a reason for her sudden gloom.

'Please don't be angry.' Blue eyes pleaded for his patience. 'I'll gladly be your housekeeper. It's just that— well—I'd always intended to play that role in Senhor Veloso's household as repayment for his kindness to me. Whatever he intended to do in the future, it doesn't put me in the right.'

'Oh, is that all?' Her concern was dismissed with an airy gesture. 'Fulfil your duties well, *namorada*, prove to me that every *cruzado* was well spent, and I'll repay the sum with interest. Will that satisfy you?'

'No!...Yes!...I don't know!' Ria flushed as Vitor burst out laughing at her vehement and contradictory reaction to his offer. 'I mean, I should like him to get his money back, but I don't want you to pay it.' She gazed at him earnestly. 'I'd only be exchanging one obligation for another—don't you see?'

'I only see you're my wife and therefore automatically under an obligation to me. What were the vows you made, hmm? To love, honour and obey? Well, Ria, love is a thing which can't be given to order, but I certainly expect to be both honoured and obeyed. Therefore, if I say I will repay Veloso I shall do so and you will accept my decision. There was only one thing I wanted from Veloso—and that I now possess.'

The tone of Vitor's reply was so stern and unyielding it was all Ria could do to repress the shiver that trembled through her body. She was used to authority, but not male authority, and now she realised for the first time that she had no idea how to deal with it. Now, her sensitivity told her, was the time to let discretion be the better part of valour. Meekly she bowed her golden head and held her tongue.

Apparently satisfied by her mute response, Vitor's brow lost its furrow as he led her through the kitchen to the bedroom.

Here again a woman's touch was much in evidence. Light shades of peach, tan and oatmeal blended and contrasted to make a restful inviting room. The bed was a small double, so plump-looking and inviting Ria couldn't resist the temptation to sit down on it. She sighed luxuriously as the well sprung mattress responded to her light weight.

'Comfortable?' Vitor gazed at her with open amusement as she bounced gently enjoying the resilience beneath her.

'Heaven!' she accorded with an answering grin. 'The convent believed in mortifying the flesh to purify the spirit. Oh, not that we slept on wooden planks,' she hastened to explain as she saw him frown. 'But we certainly didn't have sprung mattresses. The nuns would have considered them effete.'

'Were you happy there, Ria?' To her surprise Vitor came across to sit down on the bed beside her, placing one arm round her shoulders. His touch was so light she accepted it without comment, considering her answer before speaking.

'To a degree,' she admitted at last. 'I was certainly grateful and determined to make the most of what was on offer—and the education was good, very good. I was taught everything an accomplished young lady should know. Not just household management, but mathematics, languages, the arts...' She paused, unnerved by a dark indefinable glimmer she could discern at the back of the formidable eyes that insisted she continue.

What she *had* lacked was love. It was something she didn't want to admit to the forceful man sitting beside her lest he misunderstood the confession.

The nuns had been fair but distant. The other girls had been pleasant, but close friendships had been actively discouraged. To show preference for one girl's company over another's was to ensure the chosen confidante was removed to another class or study group—and she couldn't count the times when she had longed to leave the convent in the holidays to spend only a few days with the man who called himself her guardian in an effort to get to know him better in order to dispel the odd aversion she had still felt instinctively towards him—especially when, on his infrequent visits, he had actually put his arm round her shoulders. Besides, it would have been appropriate, if sad, to make the acquaintance of the ailing Senhora Veloso—so she had thought in her innocence!

But she had been told he was busy, and of course she had accepted that, smothering her mutiny, forcing herself to perform penances for her ingratitude to the man to whom she owed so much.

Even visits to the homes of her fellow scholars had been banned. With sudden belated insight, Ria saw she had been intended never to meet another man. School-girls had brothers and it had never been the design of the man whose interest in her had been coloured by lust for her to encounter them!

Ria shuddered and felt Vitor's fingers tighten on her shoulders.

'What else did they teach you, these nuns of yours? Did they tell you how to please a man...a husband?'

The hot blood flooded Ria's cheeks. Obviously Vitor was referring to the intimate side of married life, and since it wasn't going to concern her she thought the question in doubtful taste. Her chin rose a little higher indicating her displeasure.

'They taught us a woman is subject to the wishes of her husband in such matters,' she informed him stiffly. 'That—that it isn't necessary for her to enjoy what happens.' Brightly defiant, her blue eyes sparkled into his wickedly taunting face. 'A woman's fulfilment comes through having children,' she concluded firmly as if daring him to contradict her.

'And a man's in the act of making that possible, eh?'

He didn't wait for her answer, which was just as well, Ria thought, since his crudeness had left her tongue-tied. Instead he gave a low chuckle as he discerned her discomfort, getting easily to his feet and standing in front of her, hands thrust into the pockets of his snug-fitting pants.

'Dear heavens, *menina*—it's a long time since I saw a woman blush. Or can it be your white skin that betrays your feelings more easily than the olive shades of your Brazilian sisters?'

'Half-sisters,' Ria corrected, an imperious note in her quiet voice. 'My father was English.'

'Indeed? I thought you didn't know your father.' Vitor's dark eyebrows arched in surprise.

'I knew who he was!' she informed him haughtily.

'You mean you knew his nationality?'

'I knew his Christian names too!' She was angry at the tone of the question. She might have been illegitimate, but she hadn't been spawned in some downtown bordello. She had been a love-child—the fruit of an enduring passion between her beautiful mother and the blond-haired Englishman who had adored her. 'He was called Francis Bernard! I—I can't remember his last name. As my mother wasn't his legal wife she wouldn't use it. She preferred to take his middle name and call herself by that instead.'

'So.' She was subjected to a long searching look. 'Bernardi isn't your mother's maiden name. I'd assumed it was.'

'Then you assumed wrongly,' Ria told him tersely.

Her mother's name was still well known in certain circles of São Paolo society, but she, like Caterina, refused to utter it. Even now she refused to let it pass her lips, so great was her resentment towards the patriarch of the family—her grandfather who, if not the architect of his daughter's tragic death, had certainly played a major role in causing it.

She moved her shoulders in a negligent graceful movement of dismissal. 'In a city with a teeming changing population it's impossible for the authorities to keep proper records. People come and go without registration or detection. In the slums of São Paolo no one cares what you call yourself.'

'So it seems.' Thankfully Ria noted he was going to let the subject drop. The last person she wanted to discuss was her maternal grandfather. 'And since an English rose needs sustenance as much as a Brazilian peach it's high time I went out and bought some food to stock our admirable but empty refrigerator,' he told her pleasantly.

'I'll come with you!' Joyously Ria sprang to her feet, the idea of going round a supermarket an unspeakable thrill for her.

'Hey, hold on.' Vitor shot her a curious glance. 'It's only a shopping arcade I'm going to—not Disneyland!'

To someone who had only seen a supermarket through the enormous glass windows that fronted it as she had wheeled the heavily laden trolleys of the wealthy through the car park, dependent on their meagre tips for food during her mother's unemployment, the prospect of entering such a place was indeed as exciting as Disneyland.

'I still want to come!'

'No, Ria.' The harsh tone of Vitor's refusal stunned her. She opened her mouth to protest, saw the warning on his face and thought better of it. 'I want you to stay here.' One long finger indicated a chest of drawers against the wall. 'If you're bored you can put fresh linen on the bed. It's kept there. And when you've done that you can sit down and listen to the stereo.'

A little dejectedly Ria followed him back into the main room.

'I'm not sure I'll be able to work it,' she offered a trifle sullenly.

'Then read the instructions!' Stooping to a low drawer and opening it Vitor rose again, a leaflet in his hand. The petulant droop of her mouth incited his sarcasm. 'You can read and understand instructions, I assume?'

'Of course.' She smiled back sweetly, stung by his derision. 'In three languages apart from my own—French, Spanish and English.'

'No Japanese?' Something darkened behind Vitor's magnetic eyes, a stirring of something Ria couldn't give a name to behind the silky curtain of lashes that fringed them, a quality that made her catch her breath as he continued evenly, 'But then that doesn't matter, *menina*, because the only instructions you are going to receive will be in your native tongue, and since you assure me you have no difficulty in understanding that, you will make quite sure they're obeyed implicitly or you will find yourself in all kinds of trouble!'

He left her, whistling softly under his breath, while she fumed silently at the tenor of his exhortation. He was treating her like a child and an irritating one at that! Hadn't he any idea how she was feeling pulled out of a safe environment, kidnapped, pressurised into marriage with a stranger, transported to an alien place in a city she hadn't seen for six years?

'I shan't be long. Remember what I said.' With a brief wave Vitor passed her on his way to the front door. She heard it open then close and she was alone.

Of course he didn't know how she felt, she scolded herself. Why should he? Whoever he was, he showed no signs of ever having had to endure poverty. He was too slick and self-assured, too sophisticated to have learned the hard way. She was a useful tool of vengeance for a wrong the full extent of which he hadn't divulged to her, to be tolerated while she kept her place. The problem was she wasn't sure what or where that place was!

Moodily she returned to the bedroom and the duties accorded to her. The drawer disclosed a number of pure cotton sheets in pastel colours. Selecting a soft fondant peach Ria quickly made the bed, completing the job and drawing the heavy brocade cover back in place.

As she did so a framed photograph lying on its back on the top of the bedhead caught her eye. Carefully she picked it up to gaze at the face of a woman whose dark hair was piled on top of her head above a face of high forehead and wide cheekbones. An exotic face rather than strictly beautiful, but fabulously, electrifyingly attractive, Ria conceded. Lustrous eyes warm and intent seemed to dominate the photograph, although the wide shapely mouth made its own silent demand for recognition. Difficult to judge her age. Not young but definitely not old, Ria pondered; probably late twenties or early thirties, she hazarded, reading into the woman's expression the history of experience.

For a moment she hesitated before very carefully turning the frame over and undoing the clips which held it in place. The photograph fell into her hands. On the back was one word, but it confirmed what she had guessed. 'Marta'.

An odd feeling twisted inside Ria. Ache rather than pain, she defined it to her own amazement as jealousy. But she had no reason to be jealous of Vitor's mistress. She certainly didn't aim to replace her in his affections! No, it must be because Marta had an indefinable air of regality about her—a quality of leadership. Totally feminine, there was a hint of steel behind the exquisite velvet. No man would dare to insist on Marta's unqualified obedience, Ria thought rebelliously. And that alone explained her envy, even if it didn't excuse it.

Replacing the print in its frame Ria snapped the clips into position and set it upright where she'd found it. It wouldn't do for her newly taken husband to discover she had been prying into affairs which didn't concern her. Having satisfied her curiosity, she was prepared to follow the instructions he had left for her and experiment with the stereo set.

Although some of the technical terms eluded her she found the basic instructions simple and was soon rewarded with success. Curiosity made her listen to the local news bulletin before switching over to the tape-deck, but there was no announcement of her disappearance so Vitor must have been correct in his surmise that Veloso had been duped into believing she had eloped, and decided in his own interests not to publicise the fact.

Searching through the drawer of tapes, she discovered many of the classical pieces she had learned to love, but she needed something to lift her suddenly dampened spirits. She found it. What good Brazilian would be without some recording of a samba? And Vitor was no exception.

Soon the joyous rhythmic beat was filling the room as Ria snapped her fingers. She had learned to dance at school, surreptitiously in the dormitory after 'lights out', tutored by some of her more socially sophisticated friends, anxious to hand on their expertise to the quiet, popular blonde girl who seemed so alone in the world.

After a while mere finger snapping wasn't enough. Ria rose to her feet, body swaying, feet moving to the beat. She could feel the music becoming a part of her, lifting her to another realm, releasing her from the mundane. How long she danced she didn't know, replaying the tape every time it came to an end.

She was undulating, her body moving with a freedom which would have been applauded by her youthful instructors, abandoned to the magic of the music, when the door to the room opened and Vitor stood on the threshold a large carrier in his arms.

'So this is what you get up to when you're left alone, is it?'

'I wasn't doing anything wrong.' She was automatically defensive, about to justify herself further, to explain she had already carried out her domestic duties, but he gave her no chance to speak.

'Oh, yes you were.'

The carton was on the floor as Vitor hauled her into his arms.

'Didn't those sisters of yours tell you it takes two to samba?'

His hold on her was strong, almost cruel, as he brought his body against hers, taking the initiative, leading her, enticing her, allowing the music to flow through both of them, binding them together with a magic thread.

The tape ended and they were still together, the heavy thud of Vitor's heart finding an answering echo in hers. Suddenly afraid, Ria tried to break his hold.

'Please, let me go.'

She never finished the sentence, the rest of her words lost as he tangled his fingers into her wild mane of hair and discovered the sweetness of her mouth with his own.

She hadn't known what to expect after his first predatory lunge, but the mouth on her own was surprisingly gentle. Almost as if he was promising to wipe out all her doubts and fears, Vitor traced the outline of her lips with a delicate tenderness until he felt her initial resistance drain away.

Entranced by what was happening to her, Ria felt Vitor's hand leave her hair, moving lower to support her neck as his mouth grew harder and more demanding so she had no option but to open her lips. An odd mixture of alarm and excitement overwhelmed her as his other arm drew her even closer to his own body and she felt its heat transmitted to her own as his questing tongue sought a deeper intimacy within her mouth.

Tensing against such an unknown invasion, Ria found herself suddenly released, bewildered by the responses of her body—the tight, sharp ache in her breasts, the burning yawn in the pit of her stomach, a terrible weakness in her legs that had nothing to do with dancing.

For a timeless moment Vitor's dark-pupilled gaze sought hers before drifting down to regard her soft lips, parted and swollen from his kiss.

'*Mai de Deus,*' he breathed as if it were a prayer rather than an oath.

Ria wouldn't have reproached him even if she had had either the strength or the courage to do so. The exclamation merely echoed her own unspoken reactions to what had just occurred.

Then he was turning away, his voice calm and unconcerned.

'The lesson's over, *menina*. Come and help me unpack and I'll show you where everything goes.'

What lesson? Ria wondered as, smoothing her tumbled hair back into place, she followed him into the kitchen.

CHAPTER SIX

HOURS later, as Ria carefully wiped the bone-china plates and laid them lovingly back in their racks in the well fitted kitchen cabinets, she congratulated herself on the success of the meal she had provided.

Cooking in these circumstances with excellent equipment and unsupervised had been a real joy—a fun thing—and she had enjoyed every minute of it once Vitor had shown her how the electric cooker worked.

She had served *churrasco*, marinating the superb beef he had provided in a mixture of olive oil and herbs before threading it on the cooker's integral steel skewers beneath the grill. Of course she had to admit it wasn't quite the same as the real thing—cooked over hot coals or charcoal—but the meat had been tender and juicy served on its bed of rice with a side salad. To follow there had been fruit—a selection of bananas, pineapple, passion fruit and guavas.

It had been a simple meal served with wine but Vitor's appreciation had been unstinted, and Ria felt herself glowing with pride at his praise. At the convent one had been either satisfactory or not satisfactory. There had been no degree of merit, for pride was a sin.

She emitted a long-drawn-out sigh. She had long grown accustomed to the idea that she was no saint, but now as she thought ahead of the more complicated dishes she would prepare and serve with the intention of winning Vitor's approbation, she admitted her need for gratification was a fault she had no wish to eradicate.

71

He was sprawled out on the long couch studying some papers when she re-entered the room. She raised her hand stifling a yawn.

'Ready for bed?'

If she hadn't had his assurances of leaving her alone she would have been apprehensive as the mocking eyes in his olive-skinned face scanned her slender body.

'I am a little tired,' she admitted quietly. She couldn't expect him to give up the one available bed for her, so presumably she would sleep on the couch. It looked extremely comfortable and she could just imagine curling up on it. All she would need would be a cushion or pillow for her head. It was a warm night and since she had no other choice, she would have to sleep in her dress again.

'But please don't let me disturb you,' she hastened to add as Vitor swung his long legs to the ground.

'Being disturbed is something I'm going to have to learn to live with, *menina*.' It sounded like an admonishment, but there was no irritation on his bland face as he rose leisurely to his full height. 'As a matter of fact I'm ready for sleep myself.'

A statement that hardly surprised her. Although he had hidden his weariness well Ria's compassionate appraisal told her he was finding it a great effort to make his will-power overcome the demands of his body for rest. After all—he had slept for even fewer hours the previous night than she herself!

'Here——' Vitor had moved to the long low sideboard to lift a large carrier-bag from it, something she hadn't previously noticed. 'You may use the bathroom first and take this with you.' The corners of his mouth twitched at her wide-eyed surprise. 'I remembered you hadn't got a toothbrush with you, and that your wardrobe was severely limited in other respects.'

Eagerly Ria accepted the gift. The bag was large, much too big for just a toothbrush! Head bent, cheeks flushed with pleasure, she ripped off the paper covering, too excited to undo it systematically. There was indeed a toothbrush. There was also an exquisite lace-edged camisole of flesh-coloured silk that heightened the colour already invading her face.

From a distance she heard Vitor's explanation.

'I thought you'd like a change of underwear. The assistant assured me it would fit an average figure.'

The silk slithered through Ria's fingers. Never in her life had she possessed anything so beautifully sinful. It was a world away from the plain cotton undergarments she had grown used to. To own something not only functional but glamorous as well was a new kind of pleasure.

'Thank you—oh, thank you, Vitor!' Her shining eyes raised to his watchful face perceived his pleasure at her response. But he made no move towards her, merely pointing to another still unwrapped package. 'There's something else as well.'

'Yes...' Her heart pulsating with excitement, Ria undid it, revealing a negligee set in midnight blue. In heavy, opaque satin, it was simply classical. No frills or furbelows, just a plain opera top above a bodice, the curved seams of which splayed out into a tulip-shaped floor-length skirt. The accompanying coat was equally elegant, its narrow folds caught with a tie belt.

'They're beautiful!' Tears of utter joy spilled from her eyes. Furiously she rubbed them away. 'I've never owned anything like this. I never dreamed I would!'

'Not even when you knew your so-called guardian was a wealthy man?'

Ria frowned at the mocking disbelief in the dark eyes that teased her.

'I never thought of his wealth. I hardly ever saw him,' she replied truthfully. 'All I thought of was belonging to someone, being part of a family. I thought I would be like a daughter to him and his wife. I'd heard she was ill and I imagined looking after her. No one had told me she was dead!' Her voice broke as, ashamed of confessing her adolescent longings, she gathered up her clothes and made a dash through the bedroom to the bathroom beyond it.

Behind her she heard Vitor utter a curse, angry no doubt at her hysterical outburst. But there was nothing to indicate his displeasure in the words that drifted after her.

'Tomorrow we'll see about getting a complete wardrobe for you, *meu amor*.'

Bearing in mind Vitor's own professed tiredness, Ria completed her toilette with alacrity, placing her discarded clothing in the bin provided.

She spared herself a few seconds to gaze at her reflection in the long bathroom mirror after slipping the nightdress over her head, shaking her head in disbelief.

Could this really be Ria Bernardi? This female creature whose innocently unmade-up face sat so strangely over a body the voluptuousness of which was outlined and emphasised by the clinging dark satin? The garment was more like an evening-dress than a nightdress, she thought, a small smile on her lips. Only what woman would dare wear such a gown in public!

The top curves of her white breasts were starkly opulent against the darkness that draped but didn't conceal the proud peaks of her nipples. Wonderingly she allowed her hand to travel the shape of her own body, sliding down the rib cage, skimming the rounded curve of her abdomen where the satin dimpled across her shallow navel to touch lightly the long sweep of her thigh, before withdrawing it quickly, conscious of a much deeper guilt than mere vanity. As she had touched her own body she had found herself wondering what it must be like to feel a man's hands travel the same pathway.

It was something she would never experience. She was tied to Vitor, who didn't want her in that way. She was his nominal wife. But Marta was his love.

Drawing the wrap tightly across herself Ria entered the sitting-room, announcing in what she hoped was a calmly indifferent tone, 'The bathroom's free.'

'Good.' A quick smile of approval. 'It seems I've married a paragon of a wife. I expected to have to wait at least another half-hour.'

She watched him move with a lithe masculine grace into the bedroom before turning out the light, pulling a cushion down into place, and snuggling down on the couch.

Minutes later the room was flooded with light again and she opened startled eyes to see Vitor standing over her, a baleful expression on his attractive face.

'What the hell do you think you're doing here?' he grated.

He was stripped to the waist. Unwillingly Ria's bemused gaze dwelt on his bronzed torso, the smooth satin skin stretched tautly over hard muscles. As a child she had seen her male neighbours without their shirts, but the sight had never affected her like this! Surely none of them had ever looked like Vitor did at that moment— his body a perfect welding of power and beauty? Or had she been too young to notice?

Probably both, she thought as she tried to control the rapid racing of her pulse, as he stood there glaring down at her, his legs in dark pyjama trousers braced apart, his frame tall and arrogant in stance.

Studying the rigid line of his jaw Ria searched for a clue as to what she had done to upset him.

'Is there something wrong with your bed?' she ventured at last.

Penetrating dark eyes stared momentarily into hers as Vitor let out a breath of extreme exasperation. 'The only thing wrong with my bed is the fact that you're not in it!' he rasped.

A small panicky sensation rose inside her. Quickly Ria controlled it.

'I'm very comfortable here,' she assured him placatingly. 'I don't want you to give up your bed for me.'

'Which is just as well, since I'd no intention of doing so!'

His sharp voice was like a slap in the face as Ria met his hard features, a deep feeling of unease assaulting her.

'For God's sake, Ria—it may not be a king-size but it's perfectly ample for two adults!'

For you and Marta! she retorted silently, not daring to speak the words to his face. But hardly for a man and woman who were supposed to be living like brother and sister. Or had Vitor gone back on his word? Fear of the unknown tensed every muscle in her body. She had accepted his casual endearments as part of his plan—even an overture of friendship—the kiss he had given her after the wedding had only been for the sake of appearances but this afternoon, when he had returned to find her dancing, what had that meant? It had happened so naturally—a climax to the fun and excitement of the music. But it hadn't any further implication...had it?

'What's the matter, Ria?' he demanded harshly, as if he sensed the anguish behind her silence. 'Do you imagine I mean to break my word and ravish you?'

Heart thundering as the adrenalin flowed through her system, Ria looked away from his angry face. 'I— we——' she faltered miserably, lids lowered, the fan of blonde lashes casting shadows on her flushed cheeks as she took a deep breath. 'At school we were told not to put temptation in a man's way. That their d-desires were more violent than our own and less controllable, and it was up to a woman not to encourage them gratuitously.'

'Does that apply to wives, *namorada*?'

Ria flinched at the sarcasm behind the soft endearment, but she had no wish to antagonise him further.

'Not to proper wives,' she said quietly. 'It's their duty to endure their husbands' demands. That's what marriage is for. That and the procreation of children, of course,' she amended quickly.

'I see.' His voice was like dark velvet, his face as she dared to peep at it taut with barely leashed emotion. 'It seems you were taught to put great store on obedience, *menina*. So let me remind you our marriage would be considered very "proper" by those authorities you keep quoting at me. Now...' The velvet had been stripped off to reveal the steel behind it. 'Get off that couch and into the bedroom before I lose my temper. Move!'

Ria moved. Gathering her robe tightly about her, stumbling as the unaccustomed length nearly tripped her, she followed Vitor's pointing finger, keeping as far away from him as she could, until she came to a halt, her body trembling with apprehension at the far side of the bed.

'Take off the wrap, Ria.'

She stood there for a moment staring at him, saw the purpose in his eyes and did as he asked, allowing the midnight satin to fall to the floor at her feet. Every nerve of her body trembled as she recalled in vivid, cruel detail what befell the women of the *favela* when they dared to defy their men.

'Drop your hands!'

She hadn't realised how she had instinctively been shielding herself from Vitor's eyes until he barked the order at her. Tears of mortification stung her eyes but she allowed her hands to fall to her sides as his eyes raked over her.

She knew what he would see. What she, herself, had seen in the bathroom mirror. She swallowed miserably. She had already insulted him by implying he might break his word. It would be her own fault if he did.

Silently she awaited his pleasure, knowing she would make no attempt to prevent whatever was in store for her, although her whole being shuddered away from a cold-blooded invasion of her virgin body. Vitor was right. Legally and morally she was his wife and she had been taught that submission was a wifely virtue.

'Yes, as I suspected, very delectable.'

She stiffened as his slow, deep voice addressed her from the other side of the bed, thankful that he had made no move to touch her. She didn't think she could bear his fingers to follow the impertinent path his eyes had already travelled.

'But not irresistible—especially for a connoisseur of female beauty.' His soft drawl sharpened and quickened as he added abruptly, 'Now for the love of heaven, Ria, get into bed and let us both catch up on our sleep!'

Hardly believing he meant it, she slid on to the soft mattress, drawing the cover up to her shoulders as Vitor climbed beside her.

'Oh, and one more thing. I have a deep respect for the holy Sisters who raised and educated you, but I'm getting very tired of hearing their doctrines quoted at me!'

Before Ria could think of a suitable reply, Vitor had turned his back to her, flicked out a lean brown hand to extinguish the light, and ended their conversation for the night.

The sunlight was streaming into the room when Ria awakened the following morning. She stirred, luxuriating in the welcome comfort beneath her, before turning her head to discover she was alone in the bed. From outside came the delicious scent of coffee and the aroma of warm bread.

So Vitor did intend to keep his word. A warm glow of contentment seeped through her. She had been faced with an impossible decision the previous day. Her logic told her to return to the man who claimed to be her guardian, but her instinct had warned her, as it had in the past, that Gustavo Veloso was not all he claimed to be.

Heaven alone knew why she had trusted Vitor Fortunato. But she had, and it seemed that trust hadn't been misplaced. Swinging her long legs out of bed, Ria determined he would not be disappointed in her housekeeping skills.

'Your coffee's in here.' Vitor greeted her with a pleasant smile as she emerged showered and refreshed from the bathroom, fastening the sash of her robe tightly round her neat waist. 'Did you sleep well?'

'Marvellously!' Ria reached for her cup, gazing at him over its rim before raising it to her lips. 'Thank you, Vitor.'

His eyebrows rose in mock surprise. 'For letting you share my bed? It was a pleasure.' There was a devilish glint in his eyes that teased her unbearably.

'You know what I mean,' she said, watching him carefully, unable to prevent the embarrassment which coloured her cheeks.

Vitor laughed huskily. 'Yes, I know, *menina*. I must admit to finding it rather a novelty. It wouldn't be the first time I was thanked for taking positive action with a lady. It's certainly the first time I have been for doing nothing!'

Ria took a sip of her milky coffee. She would have to get used to Vitor taunting her. To a man of the world her prim reactions must be very amusing, and she was wise enough to know the more she allowed her confusion to show, the longer he would continue with his teasing.

Thoughtfully she reached for one of the rolls fresh from the oven. She had known the man sitting opposite her for such a brief period of time, yet already she was beginning to understand him, recognising how he called her alternately by an endearment and then by the nomenclature of 'child'.

She might be his wife, but he was very conscious of her comparative youth and inexperience and was prepared to respect them. Her conclusion gave her the reassurance she so badly needed in what, after all, was a highly contentious relationship!

Vitor drained his cup before rising from the table. 'I've a lot to do today, but I shan't forget to augment your wardrobe.' He slanted a narrow, saturnine grin at her. 'It's not my intention to keep you pregnant and in tatters as some men recommend as a recipe for fidelity. There's also plenty of food in the fridge and freezer and if there's anything else you particularly want, let me know.'

'But I wanted to come with you.' Disappointment welled in a deep spring as her face became woebegone. To enter the shops with their glittering fashion displays had been like the promise of paradise to her. Her needs were small, but oh, to be there, to touch the soft fabrics. Just to see all the things she had never dreamed to possess at close range! It was contrary to her nature to beg for favours, but now she did.

'Please, Vitor.' Anxious blue eyes gazed at him beseechingly. 'I promise not to be a nuisance.'

'Not yet, Ria!' She could hear his impatience. 'I don't want us to be seen together until a good many people know we are legally married. That will be our insurance of safety.'

'But I don't understand.' Ria dared to defy him. 'What danger are we in?'

'A great deal unless we're very careful! Gustavo Veloso is an evil and ruthless man. At the moment he believes you've eloped with some brash cowboy and is doubtless sending out his private army to track you both down. I've stolen something very precious from him and I don't mean him to discover where you are, or with whom, until the moment is right. Then, believe me, I shall take the greatest pleasure in letting him know to whom it is he owes his humiliation!'

Ria stared at her husband's angry face, feeling the depth of his emotion. Never had she glimpsed such bitterness in anyone's face or heard such hatred distort a man's voice.

'What did he do to you personally, Vitor, to make you loathe him so much?' she asked gently.

'It's a long story.' He was impatient but not unkind. 'One day when I'm in the mood and have the time I may tell you. In the meantime I want you to stay here in the apartment. Our future protection will be within a framework of family and friends. When I've finalised my plans our marriage will be common knowledge and even Veloso won't dare to raise a finger physically against either one of us. You'll see.'

Slowly the dark fury drained from his expression.

'Come now, *meu amor*, life could be a lot worse for you, could it not?' He waved his arm to encompass the surroundings. 'This place hasn't been lived in for some time. I'm sure you can find something that needs washing or cleaning. And if not, well, there's a bookcase full of books, and although many of them won't be to your taste, I imagine you'll find some to please you.' A sense of mischief made his eyes sparkle. 'And if all else fails— you can always practise your samba. If my plans work out as I hope you'll soon be putting your steps to the test!'

Ria watched him move to the door wishing he had been a bit more forthcoming. Only as he walked with his customary lazy elegance away from her did she realise she didn't even know what he did for a living.

Or was being a landlord and accepting rent enough to keep a man like Vitor Fortunato in the style to which he seemed accustomed? He had spoken too of a family. Where were they, and how would they react to her sudden arrival among them? Illegitimate and impoverished, she was scarcely the bride any proud father and doting mother would choose for their son!

It was too late to question him further as he sketched her a wave of farewell.

'Behave yourself, *menina*. And whatever happens— don't answer the door to anyone!'

CHAPTER SEVEN

A WEEK later she was none the wiser. Ria stood alone in the sitting-room surveying her surroundings with a petulant droop to her shapely mouth. For the past seven days nothing had changed. True, Vitor had brought her a small selection of casual clothes with the promise to provide her with more in the near future and she had been thrilled and grateful to receive them, but being cooped up was driving her mad!

Only on the odd occasion when she had been ill had she been confined to one room for any length of time in the past. She sank down restlessly on to the couch. Having discarded the greater section of books Vitor had suggested she looked through, since they appeared to deal with legal aspects of property-control, she had discovered some interesting travel books—notably one about England which she had devoured with deep interest—for wasn't she half English? But from the remaining novels she had found none enthralling enough to obliterate her mounting irritation at her forced inactivity.

Oh, what was the point of sitting around like this? She bounced to her feet again, making for the stereo, choosing some dreamy romantic film-theme music. Slowly she began to move to its rhythm, her wayward thoughts wondering what it would be like to be held closely in Vitor's arms once more.

She sighed deeply. It seemed their fraternal relationship was becoming well established. Except she doubted many brothers and sisters over the age of ten shared a bed as peaceably as she and Vitor. It seemed impossible now that she had ever been afraid of his molesting her. Wretched man! She rated him silently. He was out all hours of the day presumably satisfying his male needs with Marta! Oh, dear heavens, what was the matter with her to be so cynical? Probably making love with Marta, she amended her musings more charitably, and then wondered why that conclusion made her feel even more restless!

She stared down at her left hand, her steps automatically halting. Did Marta wear a ring—his ring? The emerald and diamond cluster stared back at her, coldly impartial. When Vitor had first presented her with it a few days previously, she had thought it an imitation. Enthusing over the fact it looked 'almost real', she had gone scarlet with embarrassment when Vitor had told her drily that if it wasn't genuine then he had been robbed by the most famous jeweller in São Paolo.

Of course, she brooded, it was just for show. Another way for Vitor to advertise his possession. He hadn't even asked her what stone she liked, simply telling her softly, 'I thought this would be particularly apt, as Veloso threatened to accuse your mother of stealing his wife's emeralds.' A comment that had given her a little more insight into his complex character if nothing else!

'Oh, Mama,' Ria spoke aloud. 'I wonder what you'd think if you could see me now.' She gave a small gulp. This was getting her nowhere. Instead of becoming maudlin, what she needed was action—but what? A sudden thought struck her. Although Vitor kept the food shelves stocked, his imagination didn't extend much beyond choice cuts of meat and the occasional pizza. For the last couple of days she had longed to be able to cook him something special; to watch with pleasure and pride while he enjoyed the labour of her hands and her heart.

What was she thinking? Heart? But she didn't love Vitor, did she? He was an attractive man—incredibly so. She enjoyed being close to him, knowing his warm vital body was within reach of hers. She felt warm and protected in his company—alone and a little scared when she was left to her own devices in his absence.

Every evening she counted the minutes until she heard his key in the lock, waited for his face to light up with pleasure when he saw her in one of the new outfits he had given her, wondered if he would sink himself deeply enough in his role of husband to drop a kiss of greeting on her upturned face. But he never touched her now, not even a quick peck on the cheek before leaving each morning, and he consistently forbore to discuss the plans he was making, merely telling her they were nearing fruition and she wouldn't have much longer to wait for the answers to all her questions.

Could it possibly be love she felt—this strange, uncomfortable feeling that persisted despite all her logic, leaving her feeling so restless and frustrated?

Quickly she moved to the stereo, cutting the music off at the touch of a switch. Vitor had a lover and she was nothing but a bludgeon to hammer home his hatred of Gustavo Veloso. The sooner she came to terms with that fact the sooner she would settle into her new lifestyle! But that still didn't alter the fact she was bored—and suddenly she knew exactly what she was going to do.

She was going to cook *vatapa*—one of the most famous dishes from the region where she had been to school. First she would need to buy the *vatapa* fish itself and some shrimps, rice flour, ginger, *dende* oil, coconut milk. She ticked off the ingredients on her fingers. And she had better get some more rice. Afterwards for dessert she would make the delicious *quindins de yaya*—the scrumptious coconut cakes that melted in one's mouth.

That Vitor had forbidden her to leave the apartment bothered her for only a moment. She wouldn't be long. Even after six years she knew where she could find the fish markets without trouble, and the other ingredients would be readily available. Half an hour at the most, she estimated optimistically. Who would bother to look at her? São Paolo was a teeming city and for some time she had begun to think Vitor was being a trifle neurotic about the vindictive nature of her erstwhile guardian!

Walking purposefully into the bedroom, she took some of the spare cash Vitor always left there, consoling herself that as it was for his own meal he wouldn't object. Pocketing the spare key to the front door she picked up a carrier-bag from the kitchen and before she could have second thoughts let herself out of the place which had been her cage for the past few days.

Once through the security gate protecting the whole apartment block and out on to the pleasant tree-lined street Ria was immediately struck by the noise of the traffic and heat of the day—both of which had been mitigated by efficient double glazing and air-conditioning in the apartment.

She stood for a few moments acclimatising herself and getting her bearings before turning off in the direction of the main shopping-centre. Dwarfed by the massive skyscrapers housing the international banks and businesses which had made the city their headquarters she was soon absorbed by the busy throng of shoppers, and before long felt her original spasm of nervousness abating.

Discovering a street market off the main avenue she soon accomplished her shopping after engaging in the customary dealing over the price asked.

Now she should return immediately, and certainly that was what she had intended, but perhaps one quick glance at the shops? It was a joy to feel the warmth of the sun on her skin and the air, tainted though it was with petrol fumes, teasing her soft blonde hair. Another ten minutes wouldn't matter, would it?

The enormous department store with its spine of steel-clad escalators beckoned her with invisible fingers. Drawn into its brightly lit, spacious ground floor she inhaled the mixed perfumes of several dozen French fashion houses, shaking her head slightly as a sales girl invited her to buy. She had helped herself to Vitor's money to purchase food. She had no intention of spending even one centavo of it on herself. '*Senhora—senhora*, just a moment if it pleases you.'

Politely Ria turned, hearing herself addressed in a woman's pleasantly modulated voice. She had wandered past the perfumery counters to the cosmetic section and the assistant who had addressed her was wearing the pale blue smock with an embroidered name-tag which announced her as being a consultant for a famous cosmetic manufacturer.

In her late twenties, elegant and lovely, the assistant was the perfect advertisement for her products, Ria decided a trifle wistfully, as the other woman smiled at her.

'Today we're offering a free trial make-up to any lady who wishes to avail herself of the offer, *senhora*.'

'Free?' Tempted, Ria let her eyes travel over the vast array of bottles and packs on display. She had never worn make-up—certainly never possessed any. To do so was to challenge the Almighty, she had been taught. For who dared to improve on God's work? She touched her bare cheek thoughtfully and saw the older woman's gaze intensify.

'Have you never worn cosmetics?' It was such a warm smile, genuine rather than practised, and Ria felt herself responding to its friendliness. She shook her head.

'Then come, sit down.' A chair was pulled out for her. 'You have an unusual fair beauty, an exquisite skin.' A professional eye was cast over her. 'You need no improvement or disguise—but just a little enhancement.'

Deft fingers smoothed a light cream into Ria's flawless complexion, drifted a touch of translucent powder over it, followed the line of her pale brows with a light brown pencil and caressed her long fair lashes with a wand of dark brown mascara. Finally a lip brush loaded with the palest of pearl pink lipsticks traced the full perfect outline of her dewy mouth.

It was only when she was finally allowed to look in a mirror that Ria realised how sensational the result was. It was her eyes, she registered in astonishment, aware for the first time in her life of just how long her lashes were and how they clashed at the corners before sweeping up and out. And the definition had made her eyes themselves look enormous, the irises bluer, the surrounding white sparkling clear! She gave a small inarticulate sound of pleasure, liking what she saw.

'I thought you'd be pleased.' Behind her the consultant gave her a reassuring smile as she handed over a small promotional beauty-pack. 'There's a sample of everything I've used, *senhora*. I hope we'll have the pleasure of your custom here in the future. I'm sure your husband will be most approving.'

Thanking her, Ria accepted the small parcel and made her way out of the shop. Talk of her husband reminded her that she had spent quite enough time away from the apartment. Vitor himself wouldn't be in for ages if he followed his usual timetable, but she wanted to allow herself plenty of time to prepare the evening meal.

She was humming softly to herself as she reached the front door. Inserting her key in the lock she opened it and entered. Her arms full of shopping she backed against it to close it then froze as the far door leading to the bedroom burst open and Vitor appeared on the threshold.

'Oh!' She gave a cry of alarm mingled with surprise as her heart slammed against her ribs. 'You frightened me!'

'As you deserve to be!' The tone of his voice, his whole aggressively held body were uncompromising. 'What the hell do you think you're up to? No, don't answer that!' He strode towards her as she gasped indignantly. She had never seen him like this before. He was so angry his body was rigid with fury, his jaw tight, his eyes narrowed, directing an icy blast at her, his fists half clenched.

Ria couldn't evade him as her shoulders were seized in a relentless grip. His breath rasping with fury he stared down into her expressive face.

'Your face tells its own story. You little fool! If you wanted cosmetics all you had to do was ask!'

Ria flushed with guilt beneath his sparkling contempt. 'It wasn't the cosmetics I went out for.'

'I noticed you helped yourself to my money.' Vitor broke across her attempted explanation. 'I thought six years in a convent would have cured you of your gutter habits. But I see you've reverted to type. It seems I shall have to remind you that virtuous young women don't steal.'

Oh, how could he be so cruel! She lifted her chin to meet his cold eyes with a sparkling challenge of her own.

'I've never stolen in my life!' Her voice sawed with raw emotion. 'Scavenged, yes. Begged, yes. Worked for it, yes. I only took enough to...'

'Put yourself in mortal danger!' There was no gain-saying his bitter condemnation as his eyes took an in-solent toll of her lovely face. 'Last month five thousand people were attacked and robbed in the streets of São Paolo. No one with any sense would dream of going out wearing a ring like the one on your finger and walking down the street unescorted. Don't you realise how vul-nerable you are? Dear God, anything could have hap-pened to you. If one of Veloso's ruffians had seen you the consequences could have been unthinkable!'

Ria glared at him, panting and flushed, as he flayed her with his tongue. All this fuss because she had wanted to cook him something nice for dinner! She glanced down at the floor where her discarded shopping-bag spilled out its wrapped contents. And he hadn't even given her a chance to explain why she had dared to ignore his instructions.

'I think you exaggerate the danger.' She forced herself to confront him with the appearance of a courage she was far from feeling. 'Besides, any sensible man would have had his wife's jewellery insured!'

'And her lovely skin as well, no doubt!' The retort came from between Vitor's clenched teeth. 'I just hope if you'd had your face slashed or been pushed under a car, the thought of my receiving compensation would have consoled you! It's just possible that Veloso would prefer to see you dead than living with me. He's no great respecter of life, I can assure you!'

'You're over-reacting,' Ria flung back stormily, making no effort to hide her resentment. 'I'm not a child, and I won't let you treat me like one.'

Disappointed because all she had wanted to do was please him and all she had succeeded in doing was bringing down his wrath on her head, Ria's angry dec-laration of independence was generated as much by her own frustration as by Vitor's high-handedness. The instant the words had left her lips she realised the extent of her mistake.

There was a short strained silence before Vitor said softly, 'Indeed, Ria? We'll have to put that to the test, won't we?'

She wanted to move, but his powerful masculine bulk was blocking her way. She swallowed a little uncertainly, unwilling to apologise but sensing words wouldn't be enough, that he would demand something more from her in payment of her sins. She didn't have long to wait.

'Get in there, Ria.' He moved away from her, his outstretched hand indicating the bedroom door.

Rage rose in her throat. A bitter, galling ache pierced through her like a red-hot poker. She had lived too long in the shanty town where everyone knew everyone else's business not to be aware of the fate that befell disobedient wives.

Somehow she had never expected Vitor to thrash her, whatever the provocation. Heat stained her cheeks and a fiery resentment burned in her eyes, but she wouldn't humiliate herself further by pleading for clemency or attempting to oppose physically his male strength. Such an effort would be fruitless and even more demeaning. Neither, she determined grimly, would she give him the satisfaction of hearing her scream—however severe the punishment he inflicted on her.

She walked, head held high, her step steady although her nerves were stretched to breaking-point.

At the far end of the room she turned to face him as he shut the door, standing against it in the stretching silence, grim dark eyes fixed on her.

'Take off your blouse.'

Ria's breath was strangling in her throat as she fought the mad pounding of her heart and the tremors that raced up and down her spine, but she obeyed him. Slim fingers slid the buttons of the short-sleeved silk top from their holes and she shrugged it to the floor.

'And the skirt.' Vitor's voice was hoarse.

Rigid pride demanded she shouldn't beg, but pain twisted across her face as she sank her teeth into her bottom lip. She wouldn't cry either. She was only going to suffer what thousands of her countrywomen suffered at the hands of their cruel, drunken husbands. Only Vitor wasn't drunk. Somehow that fact hurt more than anything else. Whatever he did to her was going to be in cold blood—and he had had the nerve to call Veloso ruthless!

Her eyes were like a wounded deer's, when having followed his further instructions, Ria lifted them towards Vitor's face. He stood there studying her, looking every inch a man without mercy, held in thrall by a mounting passion.

Deep lines grooved his mouth, his strong jaw was set, his smouldering black eyes were fastened on her as she stood there clothed only in the delicate flesh-coloured camisole that had been his gift. His handsome face was remote, unreadable. Ria knew she wouldn't have been able to reach through the aura that surrounded him even if she had tried. He was lost in a secret world of his own as his hands moved to his shirt, flinging it away from him as the buttons tore from their fastenings.

Ria shivered. It had had to be either fists or belt—and she guessed now he would use the latter. At least she thought with a cold impartiality she might be able to protect her face from the leather. It would be a pity to spoil her lovely make-up!

And then as Vitor moved towards her, she averted her face and prayed for her courage not to desert her.

She had made up her mind not to scream, yet at the first touch of his fingers she did just that. The gentle pressure against her shoulders was so alien from what she had been expecting that the shock was untenable.

Vitor seemed unaware of the harsh cry that escaped her lips. His hands strong and slender, their tan emphasised against her own paleness, were sliding the shoe-string straps down her trembling shoulders. The camisole hung suspended on the rounded curves of her breasts...and then he was pushing it away, releasing their fullness into the cups of his hands.

Ria stood motionless, knowing now that Vitor's intention had never been to beat her into submission. This had been what he had always had in mind.

Excitement curled through her as she uttered a little moan, allowing him to lead her to the bed where he sank down, pulling her on to his lap. Falling back, she was supported by his arm as his lips trailed down her throat, his warm bare chest pressing against her uncovered breasts before his mouth captured hers and his kiss became deeper, more urgent.

It was a searching, passionate act of possession, his mouth erotically persuasive as it moved on hers. A sigh of pleasure shuddered through her as every fibre of her untried body responded to the will of the ardent man who was speaking so eloquently to her, with every touch of his hands and lips.

When his mouth moved to her breasts, Ria arched her body, unconsciously offering them to his delight, squirming and panting as sensations she had never before experienced streamed through her.

Automatically her hands went to the dark head at her breast. Her fingers curled into the beautiful black springy hair tugging it gently as his tongue did impossible things to her tingling breasts. She wanted...dear heavens...what did she want? She wanted Vitor. To hold him, to absorb him, to become a part of him.

In that sweet moment of revelation she *knew* she loved him. Bending her head, rubbing her face against his hair, the skin of his neck, finding his ear and sucking on it as he was administering to the pleasure-swollen apexes of her breasts, she playfully nipped the outer ring of flesh with her sharp white teeth.

She heard his gasp then she was on her back, pinned to the bed by Vitor's hard body, and the tormented pain of desire was making his breath ragged, every gasp torn tortuously from his lungs.

She felt the strength of his arousal with wonderment and awe. She knew so little—only the basic biological facts—and they hadn't prepared her for the reality. Tentatively she ran her hands down Vitor's back, feeling the rippling muscles move beneath her fingers, a pulsing sense of adventure driving through her as he moaned.

He moved slightly, lifting himself enough to enable him to slide his hand down her nearly naked body, not content until he heard her shocked, tormented cry of mingled alarm and delight.

Ria gasped helplessly at the warm teasing provocation of his wicked hand against her untutored flesh, trapped in the mysterious web of delight and excitement he was weaving so easily around her. No one had ever told her about this kind of mind-destroying pleasure—or warned her how it could enslave her to the master-hand that conjured it.

She only knew she wanted Vitor to assuage the growing ache that was pulling her apart. As the need intensified Ria slid her hands beneath the waistband of the dark cotton trousers that clung snugly to his taut male body and dug her fingers hard into the silken skin of the hard-muscled flesh beneath them.

'Wait!' One harsh barked word and he had rolled away from her, his hands pulling at the leather belt round his lean hips. He staggered slightly, put out a hand to steady himself. The bed-head rocked and there was the sound of something falling. As it clattered on to the marble floor Vitor glanced down, then paused, buckle still in hand. Then he was stooping down, picking up the small frame and staring at the picture.

Ria caught her breath, sensing his sudden disquiet, feeling the spell between them shatter, gazing at him with dazed eyes as he uttered a harsh expletive followed by words that made her blood run cold.

'Dear God, Marta, forgive me. How could I have forgotten?'

An involuntary gasp of pain escaped Ria's parched lips. For one glorious moment she had imagined Vitor had wanted her, really wanted her, Ria, that he had fallen in love with her!

With a muffled exclamation she pulled the camisole up to cover her breasts, turning her head away from his with a pathetic attempt at dignity. What a fool she had been. How right he was to treat her like a child. It wasn't even that she'd lost him, she thought despondently. The truth was she had never even had him. He belonged to Marta. A dry sob escaped her lips.

'Ria.' Vitor had replaced the picture carefully, now he sat down on the bed beside her. His hand touched her shoulder silently, demanding she turn to face him. She took a few moments to compose herself before obeying, only to be shocked by the pale torment etched on his dark face. She could feel the anguish within him, see it in the hard tension of his muscles and the bright darkness of his eyes.

'I must ask you to forgive me.' His voice was sick with the pain of self-loathing. 'I should have remembered.'

'Please don't apologise.' She broke into his half-uttered explanation, unwilling for him to finish. She didn't want to hear him say he should have remembered Marta. Marta, whose presence was in every room of the fine apartment, whose flair and warmth gave life and depth to the stereotyped rooms. Marta who loved him so dearly she was prepared to see him married to another woman rather than contest his means of vengeance! 'It was my own fault. I was stupid going out like I did. I understand why you wanted to—to punish me.'

She stared hopefully at his forbidding face. Far better he thought she saw his lapse as a lesson for her misdeeds rather than as a preliminary to seduction. The former reason allowed him to remain her master. The latter would wound his machismo since he had given her his word.

Her stomach muscles tensed as she looked into his dark handsome face, watching his eyes deliberately take in every soft feminine curve of her figure, before he said quietly, ''When I came in and found the place empty I thought you might have opened the door to someone and been forced to leave. It was only after I spoke to the concierge downstairs and he told me he'd seen you go out alone and untroubled that I knew you'd left of your own free will.'

At the real concern in his tone Ria felt ashamed. If she had known he was coming home early she would have left him a note . . . no, that wasn't true. If she had known that, she wouldn't have gone out in the first place!

'It was the only time I've ever left the apartment,' she confessed. 'Truly, Vitor. I just wanted to buy some *vatapa* for tonight's meal.' Her voice trailed away. All this trouble over a simple piece of fish.

'*Vatapa?*' His mouth moved in an involuntary smile. 'I haven't eaten that since I left home several years ago.'

'Oh, Vitor, do you like it? The Bahian way with shrimps and coconut?' she demanded eagerly, her pleasure mounting as he moved away from her, his movements leisurely, almost relaxed. It seemed as if she were to be forgiven and that her peace-offering might be accepted.

'Very much, *menina*.' His fingers tightened the buckle of his belt and he flexed his shoulders with a hint of weariness. 'It will remind me of the meals I used to have at the *fazenda* before I was ordered to get out and not darken the plantation again with my presence until I was prepared to render unto my father the respect and obedience which was his right as head of the family.'

Scrambling off the bed, hastily donning her clothes, Ria was agog with interest at this insight into Vitor's past.

'Whatever had you done to make him give you such a stern ultimatum?' Her blue eyes were wide with incredulity.

A smile grooved his lean cheeks. 'Refused to follow the career he had planned for me, flouted his wishes on several minor points, and become involved with a woman of whom he thoroughly disapproved. All the cardinal sins a good Brazilian son must never commit.'

'The woman...' Ria's husky voice betrayed her nervousness in asking, but she was desperate to know. 'The one your father objected to—was she Marta?'

For a moment he looked taken aback, as if it had taken some extraordinary insight on her part to guess it. Had he lived so long in the apartment that he was no longer aware of how much of his paramour's influence still existed in it? Then he nodded, his face solemn.

'Yes,' he confirmed quietly. 'The woman was Marta. I gave up my home, my career and the support of my father to be with her—and I shall never regret it.'

Ria's throat felt raspingly dry. No need to ask if he loved Marta. His affection for her was in every syllable he spoke. She imagined his hands and mouth tracing the warm flesh of her own body and shuddered. She had been no more than a stand-in for his mistress. Loving him as she did, she found the knowledge insupportable.

Dare she ask why he and Marta had never married? Better not, an inner caution warned her. If his father had disapproved so much the odds were that Marta had already been married and unable to free herself from the union. Instead, after a moment's contemplation, she said, 'Do you think you'll ever go back to the *fazenda* and make your peace?'

'Most decidedly, *menina*!' He eyed her speculatively. 'That's what I came back early to tell you. All the necessary arrangements have been made for a grand reunion. You see, tomorrow is the fortieth wedding anniversary of my parents. There's to be a large celebration in the evening—over a hundred people.'

'I thought it a most apt occasion to return to the fold—to offer them my congratulations—and present my wife.'

CHAPTER EIGHT

'No!' Vitor shook his head. 'I don't like it. It's too pale—too lacking in impact.'

'*Sim, senhor.*' The patient young *modista* unzipped the gown, easing it away from Ria's shoulders with no sign of irritation.

'It was your suggestion I wear white!' Ria reproached him, her tone acerbic. 'That's the sixth dress I've tried on and you haven't liked anything!'

Seated on a small gilt chair, his shoulders hunched, his long legs splayed out in front of him, Vitor looked out of place and decidedly belligerent.

'I shall know what I want when I see it,' he grunted as Ria heaved a sigh of resignation.

She guessed the forthcoming reunion with his family was keying him up. Despite some gentle questioning over the *vatapa*, she had learned very little about his plans, saving that his father's *fazenda* was in the state of São Paolo and it would take about five hours by car to reach it. His attitude towards her had been quite amicable, but any hope that in the darkness of their bedroom she would be able to loosen his tongue proved vain, when he turned on his side and almost immediately fell into a deep sleep, occasioned no doubt by his heavier-than-usual indulgence in the white wine he had produced to accompany what had been a highly successful meal.

The only other thing she had gathered was that he wanted her to make as great an impact as possible on her introduction into society.

Her hand moved unconsciously to her hair. Shortened by four inches, treated to a body wave which had thickened and lifted it, it bounced and shimmered on her shoulders, framing her heart-shaped face with just a few tantalising wisps allowed to escape to drift across her clear forehead.

She had been astounded by the change in her appearance; hardly able to believe the metamorphosis wrought in her as she had walked out of the salon to greet Vitor who had been sitting with an iron patience waiting for her.

'Dear God,' he had breathed when he had seen her.

'You don't like it?' A wave of disappointment had flooded over her at his response. 'I thought it made me look different, older.'

'Yes.' His mouth had lifted at the corners, but it hadn't been a genuine smile, leaving his eyes untouched by pleasure as he had shrugged his shoulders dismissively. 'Don't look so despondent, *menina*. It will do.'

And now, here he was being awkward about the dress she should wear! It had been a long morning; apart from the visit to the hair-stylists Vitor had taken her around the shops buying her shoes, perfume and a set of luggage. He was a selective customer, insisting she take her time in choosing something she was really pleased with. She had certainly done that, she conceded, but now she was beginning to feel hungry.

She turned her head to look thoughtfully at the taciturn face of the seated man who had forced her into this bizarre relationship.

'Why can't I choose my own dress?' she asked with a sudden show of spirit. 'I'm not totally without taste.'

'Are you not?' It was a look of mingled humour and exasperation. 'Very well, Ria.' He clicked impatient fingers at the salesgirl as she reappeared with yet another dress over her arm. 'My wife would like to make her own selection.'

'Yes, of course, *senhora*.' The girl's face broke into a relieved smile. 'If you'll follow me I'll show you what we have in your size.'

They were model gowns, that Ria knew, one-offs in the fashionably slim model-girl sizes. It was fortunate her basic frame was slender, she admitted, because above and below her small waist her curves tended to be quite noticeable.

'This one, I think.' She turned from the rail holding a basic floor-length ivory sheath, low cut and fitted smoothly to the waist. Over it was a drift of patterned georgette silk, a riot of deep turquoise flowers thick round the hem, lessening in density as it rose higher up the bodice until only a sparse sprinkling of tiny buds lay abandoned across the line of the breast.

It was a perfect blend of purity and passion, and Ria fell in love with it at first sight.

'The senhor particularly wanted something in plain white.' The salesgirl was hesitant, biting her lip as Ria ignored her injunction and stepped into the dress.

She wasn't in any doubt of Vitor's motives, she mused a little grimly. He wanted her to appear virginal when he sprang her upon his unsuspecting parents. Well, she *was* virginal. She didn't need any white dress to emphasise her state. If her innocence didn't show on her face then no dress was going to alter the impression.

It was with a feeling of bravado that she pushed aside the curtains of the anteroom and stalked out to present herself. 'I like this one!' Her tone was uncompromising, her small chin thrust out in challenge.

There were a few seconds of silence in which she was extremely conscious of Vitor's all-assessing appraisal, then he rose to his feet with a nonchalant wave of his hand.

'Then, of course, that's the one we'll take.'

Minutes later he was thrusting her into the back seat of a taxi, piling the parcels on the seat beside her before settling his long lean length on the remaining area.

'We'll have a snack at the apartment. Something simple—pizza and coffee, for instance—and then we'll have to be thinking of leaving.' He tossed her a questioning glance. 'Did I tell you my cousin Ricardo is staying at the *fazenda* in readiness for the celebrations as my father's guest?'

'No.' Ria shook her head. Vitor knew perfectly well he hadn't mentioned anything of the kind. 'Is it relevant to anything?' She made no attempt to disguise the carping tone of her question. However devious the plot Vitor had planned, she was an integral part of it and she deserved to be told what was going on.

'Since he's going to be your official escort for the first part of the evening—very, I would have thought!' he informed her drily.

'My escort? But why? Where will you be?' Suddenly anxious, she laid a hand on his arm. 'What's happening?'

'It's like this, Ria.' His mouth was unexpectedly grim, the profile hard and forbidding. 'There's no guarantee that if I present myself at the front door I shall be welcome. My father is a proud and intransigent man. Therefore, I shall effect a less public entry. You, *meu amor*, will enter with dignity over the threshold as Ricardo's guest and be received in the style you deserve. Later, of course, there will be no doubt left in anyone's mind as to who you are, and by whose beneficence you became mine.'

'Vitor, for pity's sake!' Ria's hand tightened on his arm as she leaned closer to him. 'My guardian isn't going to be one of the guests, is he?'

'He was never legally your guardian!' Ria flinched away from the power of Vitor's response. 'He was only ever a man who saw the potential in a young female child and lusted after her for his own gratification! And, yes, Gustavo Veloso will be there. Ricardo, who is not only my kinsman but my dearest friend, has ensured it on my behalf.'

'Oh, dear God!' She paled, imagining coming face to face with the man she had accepted as having authority over her. Panic rose unbidden to her throat. What would she do? What would she say? Suppose he denounced her in front of Vitor's parents as an ungrateful, immoral jade? She swallowed hard, trying to fight the waves of nausea which threatened her.

'Don't fret, *menina*.' Vitor placed a comforting arm round her trembling shoulders. 'I would trust Ricardo with my life. While I'm by necessity unable to be with you, he will protect you in my name.'

She couldn't prevent the small shiver that trembled through her. Vitor had told her only what he thought she should know, but beneath the troubled waters he had shown her lurked monsters he had refused to reveal. She didn't know about the rest of the world, but in Brazil a man's world was different from a woman's. Few of her sex if any were allowed to cross the threshold of the esoteric fellowship that bound the male sex together. That strange land of honour and vendetta, pride and punishment, that bred men like Vitor Fortunato, her husband, was forbidden to her.

'Forgive me, Vitor.' She couldn't look at him. 'I'm scared.'

'Don't be, *meu amor*.' The deep voice was intense as he looked at her. 'All I ask is that you do as I say—and trust me.'

It was early evening before they reached the Fazenda Graciela.

'But this estate is enormous!' Ria gazed out of the window of the hired car Vitor was driving to appraise the coffee-trees which stretched away into the distance each side of the narrow road.

'My father has about a quarter of a million trees. There are larger *fazendas*.' He made it sound inconsequential.

Ria drew in a deep breath. 'And you turned your back on it? No wonder he was angry. Do you have brothers?'

'No.' The curt monosyllable rebuked her, then he added a trifle more amicably, 'I have a married sister in Portugal, but her husband has no interest in coffee either.'

'But you will inherit the plantation, won't you?'

'What's the matter, Ria? Does the idea of my being disinherited disturb you? Do you think I'm unable to create my own success in life?' He shot her a calculating look from beneath furrowed brows as the car decelerated.

'I was thinking of your father,' she answered primly, speaking only the truth. 'It must be disappointing for a man to build up something and then discover his heir doesn't want it.'

'I don't think you need worry your head about that.' Vitor brought the car to a halt before turning and giving Ria the full attention of his dark amused eyes. 'My father inherited the *fazenda* as a going concern from my grandfather who was an Italian immigrant working in the plantation. He, lucky man, fell in love with the daughter of the then-owner—a Brazilian aristocrat of Portuguese extraction. Since he had nothing more than himself to offer her, the two of them eloped.'

'Oh, how romantic!' The words were out spontaneously as Ria clasped her hands together. 'The girl's father forgave them, then?'

'What else?' The grin Vitor slanted at her was wolfish. 'To do otherwise was to admit he hadn't been able to protect his daughter, and thus detract from his own manhood. He did what all good Brazilians do in such a case—put a brave face on it in public and agreed to their marriage—and privately arranged to have my grandfather thrashed within an inch of his life!'

'Oh!' She cast Vitor a doubtful look. 'But supposing my guar—Gustavo Veloso...' She didn't finish the sentence as he interposed swiftly.

'Seeks retribution against me, *namorada*? Why, then I'll have to make sure I can out-run his bullies.' His eyes narrowed thoughtfully. 'Why the long face, Ria? Do you not think I deserve some punishment for what I'm making you endure? Don't tell me you'd shed tears on my behalf if I had to face the reckoning.'

Ria turned away from his mocking smile. 'I'd cry to see a rabbit skinned,' she retorted with cool dignity and felt his soft laughter caress her ears. There was no resemblance at all between the soft furry animal to which she had referred and the tall, hard-boned, firmly muscled freebooter who strode his own arrogant path of reprisal with little care for the consequences.

She was about to ask why they had stopped when she became aware of a figure on horseback approaching them.

'Ah,' Vitor observed with satisfaction. 'Here comes Ricardo—punctual to the minute.'

A short while later the first part of the plan had been put into action as Ricardo changed his riding-gear for the immaculate evening-suit Vitor produced from the boot of the car to take his place beside Ria at the wheel.

Now, as Vitor swung himself up into the saddle, she realised why he had remained casually dressed while insisting she dress in her full regalia for the evening ahead.

As Vitor gathered the reins in his hand and set off in a brisk gallop in a diagonal from the approach road, Ricardo accorded Ria a graceful bow of his dark head.

'While all my congratulations must be for Vitor, I would like to wish you every possible happiness in your future together.' There was a short pause while he restarted the engine and engaged the gear and the powerful car slid into motion. 'My cousin told me of your beauty,' he essayed, then added, 'Vitor is like a brother to me. I admire and respect him. He deserves all the happiness I'm sure you will bring him.'

'Thank you.' She glanced at the lean profile of her escort. Ricardo bore a definite family resemblance to his cousin. Probably a couple of years younger than Vitor, his face less stern in repose, he was nevertheless an extraordinarily good-looking young man.

Ria smiled to herself as she assimilated the newly shaved jaw, the faint lingering trace of after-shave, the luxuriance of the black hair with its hint of curl. Yes, there was no doubt of it, Ricardo was a beautiful specimen of South American manhood—and the fact left her physically unmoved.

There was no leaping of her heart, no wild careering flow of blood through her veins, no burgeoning excitement tingling through every cell of her body. If she had needed proof that it was Vitor she loved and not just his appearance, then this was it. But then deep in her heart, she had never needed proof.

'My husband told me he values you as a friend as well as a kinsman.' Ria smiled at him. Having witnessed the solid arm-clasp the two men had exchanged on meeting,

she'd had visible proof of the strength of the bond between them.

The dark head beside her nodded solemnly. 'Few men
would leave their newly wed wives with another to escort,
even though that other was already betrothed in marriage, unless their trust was absolute.' Ricardo spoke with
the pride of surety, but it was his other confession Ria
pounced on.

'You're betrothed, Ricardo? Oh, but what will your
fiancée think when you appear with me? I mean, I know
it's temporary but isn't she going to be upset?' Anxious
eyes scanned his pleasant profile.

'No,' he assured her imperturbably. 'Since she's in
England and knows nothing of the matter there's no
problem.'

'England!' Ria's heart leapt. Somewhere the other side
of the world was the possibility *she* had a family—a
father—a grandparent—cousins? 'Oh, if only *I* could go
to England!'

'Ask Vitor to take you,' came the nonchalant reply.
'Suggest it for a honeymoon if it means so much to you.
I'm sure he would indulge you.' He cast a friendly smile
at her eager face. 'Besides, you could go and introduce
yourself to Isabella and let me know if she's really as
lovely as the photograph her father sent me.'

'Isabella—your fiancée?' Surprise sharpened Ria's response. 'You mean you've never met her?'

'That's right.' Ricardo didn't seem in the least disturbed. 'Isabella's father was an old friend of my own
father before he died many years ago. He married an
English actress in Rio some twenty odd years ago and
went back to London with her. The marriage wasn't successful. There was a divorce and he kept custody of the
only child. By then he had business interests in England

but he's always wanted Isabella to return to her homeland and marry a Brazilian.'

'So you offered to make his wish come true?' Such things happened Ria knew. Somehow she had expected a girl brought up in England would have her own say about the matter. Unless, of course, she hadn't been told about her father's plans.

'Why not?' Ricardo shrugged. 'I've known her father for many years. We have a sound business and personal relationship. The match is ideal. Isabella's still finishing her education and has become quite beautiful—or so I'm led to believe. Unlike Vitor, I've no pre-conceived ideas about arranged marriages not working—but then, hopefully, Isabella isn't as spoilt as Felicia is.'

'Felicia? Who's Felicia?'

A quick look at her shocked face, then Ricardo was stifling an oath. 'I thought you would know, Ria. I assumed Vitor would have told you.'

'Obviously an oversight.' Ria forced herself to speak calmly. Marta…Felicia…Was there no end to the women in Vitor's life? 'Perhaps you'd be kind enough to repair it.'

'Vitor should be the one to tell you.' Ricardo managed to look shamefaced. 'But, well I guess it's all right in the circumstances.' He heaved a sigh. 'You see, my uncle was anxious to see Vitor married. He wanted heirs for the *fazenda*, particularly as Vitor showed little interest in coffee-growing. But in those days neither my cousin nor I was keen to settle down.' He flashed her a quick look which spoke volumes, but not as much as the faint hint of colour rising beneath his olive skin.

So he and Vitor had been a little wild in their youth. She was neither surprised nor shocked.

'Go on,' she encouraged lightly as ahead of her she could make out a blaze of light and colour through the veiling lacework of overhanging trees. 'So your uncle arranged a marriage between Vitor and Felicia?'

'She was the daughter of a neighbour, very lovely to look at; clever and cultured too. Everything my uncle wanted in a daughter-in-law. Added to which she was very much in favour of the idea herself originally.'

'You mean she was in love with Vitor?' A definite spasm of jealousy struck a pang in Ria's heart. 'What happened?'

'He met Marta—what else?' This time there was a gentle smile on Ricardo's handsome face. 'You know about Marta, of course.'

'Of course.' Ria inclined her head. She hadn't been told—but she knew.

Ricardo shrugged his shoulders. 'Felicia begged Vitor not to have anything to do with her. She warned him no good could come of their association, but Vitor wouldn't be swayed. Felicia was very angry. She'd set her heart on becoming mistress of the *fazenda* and saw Marta as a threat to everything she'd planned.' He pursed his lips thoughtfully. 'The day Vitor decided to leave the *fazenda* he fulfilled his obligations to Felicia and asked her to marry him. She refused, but she told him that one day when he'd grown tired of Marta's passion and determination he'd come crawling back to her and beg her to wear his ring again and when he did she'd laugh in his face.'

'Is she still so angry and unhappy?' Ria asked faintly, the huskiness of the question betraying her feelings more clearly than the words.

'No.' Ricardo laughed. 'She soon came to terms with the fact that Vitor never cared for her. It was a convenient arrangement, nothing more, although,' he added more soberly, 'she's never formed another liaison as far as I know. Fortunately, time has now healed the original coolness between the two families and Felicia's father is convinced she has had a lucky escape.'

The car had drawn up to large iron gates and was now being driven slowly across their threshold. Ricardo leaned out of the window and sketched a greeting to the two men at the gate who waved him through.

Ria sat in silence evaluating what she had just been told, staring unseeingly out of the window as Ricardo manoeuvred the large car into a parking-space.

Gallantly he alighted, and walked round and helped her out. Taking his proffered arm she allowed him to lead her round to the back of the sprawling main building. Here there were tables laid out beneath the trees on an extensive patio; coloured lights swung in the light evening breeze and the insistent rhythm of a samba filled the air with a pulsing excitement. People were standing around in groups or dancing, white-coated waiters moved deftly among the crowds. Everywhere there was life and laughter. Except in Ria's heart. There, there lingered only a deep foreboding—a painful jealousy.

'The idea is we mingle—get lost in the crowd.' Ricardo took her into his arms, as unresistingly she followed his lead weaving among the other dancers. 'The time to introduce you to your host and hostess will come later. Vitor will be making his own way in—evading the guards on the gates.' Ricardo scrutinised the pale face of the young girl in his arms and misread her trepidation. 'Don't worry,' he assured her readily. 'He knows this place inside out. He'll come to no harm.'

'Ricardo,' Ria gathered her courage in both hands. 'Is Felicia here?'

Her companion looked uncomfortable as he glanced around him. 'I imagine so. The two families are still on friendly terms, as I told you.'

This was going to be even harder, but she had to know. Vitor had given up Felicia for Marta, given up his family for Marta, and now she, Ria, had supplanted Marta in his life but not his affections.

'And Marta?' she queried softly, her voice low and husky, not far removed from tears. 'Will Marta be here tonight?'

She felt his shock. It ran through his lithe body like a charge of electricity, so that he missed the beat of the music and came to an abrupt halt.

'Dear God, Ria!' The young face was that no longer. It was a man's hard countenance that met her questioning stare. 'I thought you knew. Marta's dead!'

CHAPTER NINE

'DEAD!' Ria's horrified cry expressed the depth of her shock. 'But when—how?'

'I don't think it's my place to tell you.' Ricardo regarded Ria's pale face, indecision masking his darkly lashed eyes. 'I would have thought that Vitor...'

'Certainly.' Ria allowed herself to be led once more into the dance aware that the way they had stopped so suddenly and appeared to confront each other had drawn unwelcome attention to them. The awareness of Ricardo's embarrassment at being the cynosure of all eyes gave her an idea. 'And I'm sure Vitor would have told me everything if we'd had more time together. But now the subject's been broached, who better than yourself to put me in the picture?' Then as she saw him begin to shake his head she gave him her sweetest smile. 'Unless you want me to make a scene—cry out that you molested me? I imagine Vitor would find that harder to understand than your merely giving me a little background detail.'

A wry smile twisted her partner's firm mouth. 'Since you leave me no choice, then...' He shrugged his shoulders. 'It's no secret. When Vitor left university he turned his back on coffee-production, much to my uncle's disgust, to take up law. After the initial breach between them things improved as Vitor went from success to success, specialising in conveyancing and property negotiations.' Ricardo's dark face lit with humour at his memories. 'In those days Vitor worked hard and played even harder. Then suddenly everything changed. It all

112

started one day when he went to a legal seminar held in Rio. I don't think he had the slightest idea of doing anything other than wining and dining and . . .' he hesitated, obviously discomfited by what he had been about to say, but Ria brushed his silence aside.

'And having temporary liaisons with women, yes I understand the situation, and . . .'

Ricardo sighed. 'He met Marta. Like himself, she was a lawyer and similarly she had specialised in property, but there the likeness ended. Marta was a member of a group of lawyers who had banded together to give free help and advice to the poor and repressed farmers in the north-east.

'What she had to say really shook him up. Life had been so cushioned for him, his road to success so lined with the good things that a wealthy background can provide, he'd never paused to consider whether he owed a duty to those born less fortunate than himself. Or, if he did, how best he might discharge it. But Marta ended all that. She opened his eyes to a misery he'd never spared a thought for. Property developers closing down a whole fishing-village in order to build a holiday complex for foreign tourists, farmers being forced to pay fifty per cent of their profits back to the landlord instead of the statutory ten per cent, men being forced to work for a mere pittance by modern slave-drivers who thought nothing of burning down the cotton crop or their homes if they dared to resist.'

'But if the law protected them?' Ria interrupted with a frown.

'In theory it did. But in practice many were too frightened or too ignorant to invoke it. Even with the support of the Church and the Movement for Land Reform, often when they were given a just decision it proved impossible to implement.'

Ricardo sighed, gazing down into Ria's lovely troubled eyes. 'Marta was a lady of fire and passion—the material heroines are made from—and she completely won Vitor to her side. He left the *fazenda*, moving up north to Fortaleza to be with her, giving his services free, living off accumulated earnings and the private income he had from his grandfather. For two years they worked in a common cause together. My uncle was furious. He accused Vitor of embracing communist doctrines and ordered him to choose between his allegiance to his family and Marta.'

'How did she die?' Ria asked softly, tears not far from her eyes, as she imagined the painful trauma Vitor must have endured. She remembered the lovely face in the photograph back at the apartment and almost cried aloud at the stab of jealously that pierced her heart. She had been jealous of Marta when she had thought her alive. To envisage her lifeless, lost for ever to the man who had given up a whole part of his life for her, increased her anguish a hundredfold. Yet she had to know everything.

'It was about a year ago.' Ricardo's slow controlled speech was in direct contrast to the lively rhythm that washed around them, the chatter and laughter of the other guests. 'Judgement was given against one of the biggest offenders—a man with enormous property-holdings in the impoverished areas. That man was——' he paused momentarily before saying in that instant what she had guessed, 'Gustavo Veloso.

'There was a lot of rejoicing that night and the tenant farmers started putting up fences round the plots the law had given them a right to rent. Veloso sent his heavy mob in. They rode their horses through the cotton-fields, mercilessly destroying the plants. They set fire to the bales of cotton in the sheds and tied ropes round the newly erected fences and tore them down.

'The farmers and their families protected themselves, but they'd only got forks and spades. Veloso's men had guns. In the melee that followed three people were shot dead. One of them was Marta. She'd been there with the farmers congratulating them on their victory when Veloso's thugs arrived.'

'Oh, dear God—was Vitor with her?' Ria's distress was hardly audible.

'No. When he heard what had happened he swore he wouldn't rest until he had avenged her. You see there was little the law could do. Official policy at the time was to play down the land riots. The men who did the shooting were entitled to carry weapons and no one could prove the deaths hadn't been accidental. They were taken to court but only had to face minor charges. The government bought the land from Veloso and took over the role of landlord so the farmers pay only the legal rent. In a matter of months the whole tragedy was forgotten.'

'Except by Vitor.'

'And the widows and families of the other men that were killed.' Vitor moved imperceptibly nearer the edge of the dance-area, taking Ria with him. 'Vitor has always sworn that Marta's death was no accident. That Veloso wanted her out of the way and that the shot which killed her was fired deliberately. He has sworn to avenge himself on her murderer. The man on whose instructions the shot was fired.'

'Ricardo?' It was little more than a whisper that the dark-haired man had to lean forward to catch. 'Am I really such a treasure that stealing me from Veloso will wipe out such a debt? Wouldn't justice have been better served if Vitor had destroyed me as he suspects Veloso destroyed Marta?'

'Dear heavens, how you're trembling!' Ricardo seized both her hands in an effort to calm their tremors. 'You must know Vitor would never hurt you.'

But the trouble was she didn't know! If only she could be as certain as her loyal companion of the altruism of Vitor's motives. What had he said—'The day I meet Veloso face to face with you on my arm is the day I shall have claimed a major debt.'

And when the debt was publicly discharged what then? What plans did the grief-stricken avenger have in mind? 'Forgive me, Marta,' he had begged the day he had been on the point of claiming her, Ria, as his wife. That simple prayer told its own story.

Vitor still mourned his beloved Marta in whose shadow she, Ria, would always dwell. She loved the arrogant, courageous man who had stormed into her life—more now than ever after what she had learned about him. Yet that same story had confirmed what she'd already feared. Her love for him was doomed, must remain unspoken or be rejected. There was no way she could compete for it with the beautiful, tragic Marta whose influence remained from beyond the grave.

The music stopped. There was a muffled roll of drums and the lights surrounding a small raised area on the terrace glowed brighter. Ria felt Ricardo's hand tighten against her arm.

'This is my cue,' he whispered into her ear. 'Stay where you are when I leave you.'

He had hardly finished speaking when a tall, well built man in his mid-sixties stepped into the light. Turning slightly, he beckoned an elegantly dressed woman some five or six years his junior to stand beside him.

Ria's breath caught in her throat. These were un- doubtedly her unknowing hosts—Vitor's parents. Her surmise was confirmed immediately as the man began to speak in a deep pleasant voice, addressing the crowd of people who had gathered.

'On behalf of my wife and myself I want to welcome you all to the Fazenda Graciela on this happy occasion. Thank you all for coming and for the good wishes that have been expressed so warmly to both of us.' He put his arm round his wife's shoulders as she smiled up into his dark face, her eyes full of such warm generous loving that Ria felt a deep ache within herself at their so ob- viously shared affection.

'Our day has been made even more blessed by the news from Portugal that our dearest daughter Cecelia has given birth to her first child—a son—and that mother and child are doing well.'

There was spontaneous applause and a murmur of de- light soughed through the group of attentive people. Senhor Fortunato smiled. 'So all that remains for me to say now is that hot food is about to be brought out for your delectation. The night is young—enjoy yourselves!'

There was a quick reassuring pat on Ria's shoulder, then Ricardo was moving forward fast, taking his uncle by the arm, resting his hand lightly on his aunt's shoulder, capturing the crowd's attention as his strong voice rose above their chatter.

'I'm sure I speak for all of us when I thank my uncle and aunt for tonight's celebrations and express my grati- tude to both of them for their generosity and friendship, not only tonight, but throughout the years we've been privileged to know them.' He paused to allow the warm burst of clapping to subside.

'I'm as delighted as they are to know of Cecelia's joy and I have one more surprise for them.' Turning his head towards the shadows, he said simply, 'Vitor...'

Vitor Fortunato walked coolly and calmly forward to join the small group of people beneath the lights, while a universal sigh rose and faded from the watchers leaving an air of electric expectation. There was no one present, Ria guessed, who didn't know of the estrangement between father and son. Wearing dark dress trousers and a light jacket, his face drawn and sombre, each arrogant curve of his beautiful profile stark in relief against the darker background, Vitor extended his hand to his father.

There was one dreadful, poignant moment which seemed to stretch to eternity, then the older man had taken Vitor's hand and drawn him firmly into his arms as both men exchanged the *abraco*, the warm emotional embrace of close friends.

Turning from his father Vitor hugged his mother, on whose face tears of joy were unashamedly flowing. It was a very public reconciliation full of feeling and drama, and the guests were loving it, pushing forward to get a better view of the reunited family.

For a moment Ria took her gaze away from Vitor, sweeping her eyes round the assembly. There, towards the edge of the crowd she could see Gustavo Veloso. Too far away to discern his expression she could only see he wasn't smiling. Hastily she tore her eyes away, only to have them attracted to a movement in the crowd. A stunning beauty in a flame-coloured dress, her black hair elaborately pinned to the top of her lovely head was easing her way through to the front, her lips parted in happy eagerness as a pathway was made for her to reach the centre of the action.

At that moment Vitor's voice drew her attention back to him. 'I couldn't come to this celebration without

bringing my parents something very special, something
they've wanted for a long time now.' He paused as the
brunette beauty reached the front. His voice dropped to
an intimate whisper, but in the stretching silence a pin
dropping would have been heard. 'Ah, Felicia—as one
of my oldest and dearest friends I know you will share
my happiness.' One strong hand drew her to his side.
'To all of you, but particularly to you—Mama, Papa—
I wish to introduce my wife... Ria!'

Ria remained motionless, transfixed by the sick shock
she had seen on Felicia's face. Oh God, that had been
cruel. The girl's hands were twisting together, the light
reflecting from the ring she wore. Vitor should have told
her, Ria, exactly what he meant to do. She had never
dreamed he would stage a public showdown. Frozen to
the spot, she made no move to join him.

'Ria.' This time he spoke her name more gently as
hundreds of heads craned towards the shadows where
she was standing. Behind her she heard Ricardo urging
her forward, felt his hand guiding her, then she was
walking towards Vitor's outstretched hand, her head
high, her face pale above the flowing georgette of her
gown.

The arm that encircled her waist was firm and steady,
giving her the support she needed as the staring faces in
front of her became a blur.

'And for my good fortune I have to thank Senhor
Gustavo Veloso, who assumed the role of Ria's guardian
when she was a child and made her the beautiful woman
she is today.' He was holding everybody's attention as
his deep tones echoed round the terrace. 'He is here by
special invitation so that I may thank him publicly for
everything he has done—to make this union possible.
As most of you know, he is a respected family man,
although sadly recently widowed, whose gifts to charity

have always been widely publicised.' He paused to allow the buzz of noise to die away. 'A few days ago I took from him the most precious gift of all—the beautiful young woman—the existence of whom his modesty forbade him to mention in public, and to whom he intended to offer a rich and fulfilling role in his own household. I want to assure him that whatever he intended to endow her with I mean to match—if not exceed.

'For six years he nurtured a child until she turned into the lovely young woman she is today, little knowing the name of the lucky man who would one day claim her for his bride. Today it is my pleasure to make that knowledge public.'

A quick signal of his hand and the lights faded as the samba band restarted playing.

The lights were still fading. It was too dark to see where she was going. Ria stumbled, felt Vitor's start of agitation, a muffled curse, then she was in his arms, her face pressed against his shirt, and she couldn't tell if it was her own pulse that drummed so violently between them or his heart. She only knew Vitor had her safe in his arms and was striding away from the noise and clamour.

Seconds later she realised she was being carried upstairs and eventually felt herself put down on a soft bed in a dimly lit room. She closed her eyes, letting the waves of weakness wash over her until she felt better.

'It's not healthy to faint as often as you do, *namorada*.' The deep familiar voice chided her warm with affectionate amusement. 'We shall have to have you tested for anaemia.'

'I didn't faint!' Ria sat up protesting vigorously, pushing her tumbled hair away from her face. 'I just felt unwell. Oh, Vitor, how could you do such a thing? It was embarrassing and cruel!'

'I thought it went off very well.' He tossed her a wicked grin, his teeth white against the hard tanned flesh of his face as he sat down beside her, a mischievous satisfaction oozing out from every pore. 'My parents were clearly overjoyed—my mother is still weeping.'

'As I suspect Felicia is too,' Ria retorted coldly. 'Ricardo told me she was your fiancée before you walked out and left her. Dear heavens, Vitor, I saw her face! She probably thought you had come back to renew your relationship, and you even made her stand beside you while you humiliated her!'

'Did I?' His mouth quirked at the corners. 'How angry you are with me, *namorada*. She came of her own free will to stand beside me. As for humiliating her, if that is what occurred, then she must be responsible for her own degradation. Three years ago I asked her to be my wife, to come and live and work with me, to share my ideals—and she turned me down—a circumstance I've never ceased to be grateful for!' His beautiful mouth was drawn into a hard cruel line. 'Felicia's beauty is only skin-deep. All she ever wanted from me was wealth, position and an unlimited licence to enjoy herself without care or responsibility.'

It was a hard indictment. If Ria hadn't been told about her husband's association with Marta she would have contested it heatedly. Instead she raised her head and gently touched the hard lines of Vitor's jaw.

'I asked Ricardo about Marta,' she ventured softly. 'I wanted to know, Vitor. I—I insisted he told me.' She couldn't help her voice breaking.

'Poor little Ria.' The brittle line of mouth relaxed as Vitor raised his own hand to capture hers where it lay against his skin. 'I've treated you very badly, haven't I?'

To her astonishment he turned her hand, pressing the palm to his mouth. 'But at last the past is dead and can be buried. This evening when I saw Veloso's face I knew without doubt I'd achieved what I set out to do.'

'As did everyone else present,' Ria confirmed, her tone shaded with pain at the memory of what had been more of an ordeal than she had anticipated. 'I hadn't expected quite such a powerful dénouement.'

'Had you not?' Grim amusement brought an extra sparkle to his liquidly beautiful eyes as Vitor met her affronted regard. 'But I had to ensure he wouldn't trouble us in the future. As it is, I've left him with a patina of dignity by the inference that he had consented to our marriage. He'll want to hold on to that. By contesting it, or harassing either of us he will announce himself in public as the lecherous hypocrite he is.'

He released her hand, rising with languid grace to stand contemplating her. 'And now, my sweet wife, your new in-laws are waiting anxiously to receive a more private and intimate introduction to their freshly acquired daughter.'

He saw her shiver of trepidation and smiled. 'Don't let the prospect worry you, *meu amor*. They'll make you very welcome. My father and I have seldom seen eye to eye in the past but he's a fine man and my mother is the angel he deserves.' A trace of laughter lent his countenance a devastating charm making Ria's heart beat faster. 'Despite the fact that Papa is a wealthy landowner, he's also a fair one and I respect him for it. The plantation is efficiently run and the workers well provided for, with homes and a school for their children. They also have a share in the land, each owning an area for his own cultivation. So you see, he is not such an ogre as you may have supposed.'

'Yet you want no part in his business?' Ria gazed into his personable intelligent face, understanding the disappointment his father had felt. In this country a man still wanted sons to inherit his land, to carry on the family name. Vitor had denied his father the satisfaction of seeing his son follow in his footsteps as a *fazeindera*. Unless Vitor should disavow his early undertaking to herself, he also intended to deny him the joy of grandchildren.

A careless shrug of his broad shoulders confirmed her assertion. 'My father has long since come to terms with the fact that the law is my chosen career, although...' he rubbed his jaw thoughtfully, 'I may yet surprise him with the extent of my ambitions.'

He allowed the sentence to drift into silence.

'You're going to turn your back on the law?' Ria queried softly, sensing his unspoken uncertainty about his future. She was his wife after all. Surely she was entitled to know his future plans—especially since they might concern her.

'Not for a couple of years anyway, and then...' he hesitated as she waited expectantly, 'the fight against exploitation must go on, Ria. Enormous strides are being made by the government and they have to be encouraged.'

'We're going back to the north-east?' Her eyes sparkled with enthusiasm. 'Oh, Vitor, I should love to be able to help!'

She stopped as he shook his head firmly. 'No, that's not my intention. There are many as able as I am to carry on the fight *in situ*, Ria. For me there may be another way—although naturally my help would be given freely if sought. But these past days I've been renewing acquaintanceships with old colleagues.' Again he paused, his dark eyes shadowed beneath the broad sweep of his brow.

'It's a long road ahead, Ria, but stricter and more easily enforceable laws against predators like Veloso are the only long-term answer. The fact is I've joined a partnership in a legal practice in São Paolo and mean to spend a few years re-establishing myself as a proficient and reliable lawyer—rather than the renegade I'm now assumed to be!' His smile acknowledged his reputation but didn't disguise his pride at the disreputable title. 'After which time I shall consider standing for election to the Chamber of Deputies, and if successful, shall hope to bring further reforms about through the democratic action of Congress.' His dark head moved in wonderment as Ria gazed at him with unmitigated admiration. 'I've been astonished at the amount of support already pledged to me.'

'It sounds exciting, Vitor!' Ria was watching a man held in the thrall of burning ambition and the power of his determination was firing her own enthusiasm. Anything Vitor undertook would be brought to a dramatic climax. Hadn't she ample proof of that herself? His means might be devious, she admitted, but she was beginning to allow his motives were a great deal more moral than she had first supposed. 'So we'll be returning to the apartment at São Paolo?'

'Not immediately. My parents are bound to want us to spend a little time with them first. It would be a discourtesy to refuse. Afterwards, well, we shall see.' He looked down at her eager face. 'And it will be a discourtesy if we keep them waiting any longer to accord a proper welcome to their daughter-in-law.'

Reluctantly Ria rose to her feet, smoothing down the flimsy fabric of her dress, pushing her fingers through her disarranged hair. Panic was a knot in her throat, a lump in her chest restricting breathing.

'Suppose they don't like me, Vitor?' She licked her dry lips. 'They wanted you to marry Felicia, didn't they? What are they going to think when they find out I'm no fine lady, but an illegitimate waif rescued from a shanty town?'

'What should they think?' Dark eyebrows lifted in mock amazement. 'They will believe I took one look at your glowing loveliness and fell hopelessly in love.'

'Vitor, please!' Ria laid a trembling hand on his sleeve. 'I want to know the truth. I understand why you wanted to hurt Veloso, but the arguments you had with your father...the row with Felicia...' She swallowed, desperately trying to control the tremor of her voice. 'I can't help wondering if you saw the alliance between us as a way to take your revenge against them too. I'm afraid—afraid I'm being paraded in front of them as a slap in the face.' She saw his brows darken, his eyes narrow, but continued with a grim determination spilling out her deepest fears. 'They wanted so much for you, Vitor, and I can't help thinking you are taking some deep delight in showing them you have deliberately chosen so little.'

She couldn't go on looking at him, turning her head away to hide the shimmering tears from his probing gaze. Just when she thought she would receive no answer, that she had hit upon the truth and Vitor wasn't going to deny it, he spoke to her.

'Come here, Ria.'

Hesitantly she turned her head to look at him before obeying. With firm hands he led her towards the mirror.

'Look in there, Ria. What do you see?'

He had asked her the question before but had supplied his own answer. Now he waited for her to answer him.

'A girl,' she faltered. 'Fair-haired, young, inexperienced—afraid...'

He swung her round, sweeping his arms about her waist, lifting them upwards to draw her tightly into his embrace. His mouth met hers with passion and sweetness blended into an irrefutable delight.

As her lips responded to his ardent salute, Ria felt his hands rise against her back, touch the naked skin of her shoulders above the exquisite dress and thread themselves through her hair, trapping her head so that she couldn't have escaped the ardour of his kiss even if she had wanted to.

She had no such wish. His nearness, the solid presence of his strength offered the support she so badly needed. Her arms encircled him, fingers reaching to caress his shoulders, firmly muscled beneath the white tuxedo, moving upwards to run through the crisp black hair so alien yet so attractive to her own genre.

Ria's pulse began to beat wildly as every cell of her straining body thrilled to his caresses and a strange vibration stirred through her—unsettling yet exciting.

She felt the hot blood colour her cheeks, recalling how Vitor had looked at her in the apartment when he had ordered her to strip. Was it possible he might change his mind about keeping their marriage platonic after all? If she had been wrong in her assumption that he aimed to thwart his father in every possible way, wasn't there a slender chance he might want to fulfil his familial obligations?

It wasn't necessary for a man to love a woman in order for him to make love to her. Men could make love easily when they were aroused, she had been taught, and nature itself was a great instigator of passion. Even loving Marta as he still did, might not the time come when he would want to consummate their marriage?

Ria's hands tightened as she pressed her body against Vitor's hard male contours, her imagination racing. If Vitor wanted her she would go to him joyously—touch him, absorb his scent, accommodate the powerful sinew and muscles of his body with a deep love and satisfaction. In those blissful moments of culmination she would persuade herself that he loved her too.

The marriage vows were binding. If Vitor wanted heirs it was to her he would have to turn. And she would bear him a son. A strong beautiful boy who would grow up in his image, who might fight and oppose him, but who would give him undying love and loyalty like she herself would.

She knew her breathing had quickened, felt the radiant heat of her face and looked anxiously at Vitor as he slowly brought the amorous salutation of her lips to a close, standing back to look at her flushed appearance with every sign of satisfaction.

'Well, well, *menina*,' he said softly, his dark voice husky and amused. 'What a change we have here.' He lifted one hand to run the bent thumb gently over the full ripe curves of her lips, while she regarded him from eyes darkened by the languor of desire, unaware of how clearly her dilated pupils betrayed her wanton thoughts. 'Look in the mirror again, *meu amor*, and tell me what you see.'

Obediently Ria turned from him to confront her own image, uttering a small cry of shame as she met the slumberous eyes and pleasure-satiated mouth of a woman aroused by the touch of her lover. 'The same girl,' she whispered, and knew she lied.

'Oh, no,' Vitor corrected her gravely. 'That's no fearful girl who stares back at you with such distrust, my lovely. That is Frances Maria Fortunato—wife and consort of Vitor Fortunato—a man who would never extort vengeance from anyone he cared for.' His tone became brisker as he moved away from her side. 'And now you will oblige me by not keeping my parents waiting one moment longer before they can enjoy your delectable company.'

CHAPTER TEN

IT WAS Vitor's mother who came across to greet her as he ushered her into a small room which appeared to be some kind of study. But Ria paid little attention to the book-lined walls as Serena Fortunato approached her, arms extended, her lovely face lit with an inner warmth.

'Nothing could have made this day more perfect for me than to be able to welcome my son's wife to our home—his home.' She kissed Ria on each cheek, leaving an impression of a faint elusive perfume as she stood back to catch Ria's hands in her own. 'Your home, my dear.'

'You're very kind,' Ria faltered, recognising the sincerity of the greeting. It was more than either of them deserved, having deprived Vitor's parents of the privilege of being present at their wedding ceremony. That they were prepared to forgive such a breach of established custom was surely an indication of how much they both cared for Vitor, despite the yawning gap of time since he had last crossed their threshold. Or had she been too optimistic in supposing Vitor's father would be as forgiving?

As soon as the older woman released her hands and turned to embrace her son, Ria allowed her gaze to rest on the stern face of Gregorio Fortunato. Powerfully built, his dark hair winged with silver at the temples, he was regarding her with a thoughtful frown marring the broad sweep of his forehead.

'Our original introduction was rather unexpected and also very brief.' His voice had the deep timbre that had

reproduced itself in his son. 'Vitor named you as "Ria".
Do I assume you bore your guardian's family name?'

'No, Senhor.' Ria met his autocratic regard with
dignity. 'I was named Frances Maria Bernardi.' She held
her silence as dark eyes swept in a cool assessment over
her, unwilling to volunteer her history, and unspeakably
relieved when she felt Vitor's supporting arm placed
firmly round her shoulders.

'I trust my wife is as welcome at the Fazenda Graciela
as you led me to believe I was?' The words were polite
enough but there was a harsh quality of challenge beneath them as Vitor squared up to the older man.

'You gave me little option, *meu filho*, but to welcome
you,' Gregorio returned drily. 'Your reappearance was
so public and theatrical and timed on such an auspicious
occasion that to turn my back on you would have made
this family the cause of gossip for many months, besides, of course,' he paused to make a brief inclination
of his head towards Serena, 'breaking your mother's
heart.' The sombre gaze returned to linger on his son's
face. 'You took advantage of my charity and my pride,
Vitor.'

A cold tremor of apprehension ran down Ria's spine
at the cool response, but a quick glance at her husband's
face showed him not to be unduly taken aback.

'Both of which you have in abundance, Papa.' There
was a trace of amusement in the younger man's reply.
'But even then I was cautious enough not to present
myself at the front door, in case you had given orders
I should never be readmitted to the family home.'

Gregorio Fortunato shook his head. 'All I ever wanted
for you was that you should fulfil your potential to the
utmost. Perhaps I spoke too rashly at the time. I seem
to recall the atmosphere between us grew very heated.'
He shrugged his shoulders. 'The truth is, *meu filho*, I

would never have refused to see you—I assumed you had no further time for us.'

There was a moment's silence before Vitor said quietly, 'I had so much to do and I was so far away...'

'We heard about Marta's death—oh, *meu querido*, how you must have suffered!' Serena squeezed her son's arm. 'We understand that...that...' she stopped, obviously ill at ease, glancing at Ria.

'That Gustavo Veloso was at the back of it?' Vitor pre-empted his mother's suggestion. 'So he was.' Ria felt his arm tighten round her shoulders. 'I'm afraid I have to confess that Ria is my wife without the formality of her guardian's blessing. She was, in fact, as much a potential victim of his greed as Marta was.'

'I see.' Gregorio's frown deepened. 'I assume that explains why Ricardo was so insistent he should be invited tonight despite my reluctance to extend such an overture of friendship to him, and also why, after your little melodrama, he left before I had an opportunity to speak to him.'

'Oh, you poor child!' Serena's interruption was full of compassion. 'Whatever misery you've been made to undergo in the past is all over now you have Vitor to love and protect you.'

'Not only Vitor.' Gregorio came forward, his hand extended. 'You are one of us now, Ria. I know I speak for my nephew too, when I tell you that all the men of the family will be ready to defend you should the need ever arise.'

Ria took the strong handclasp extended to her, then unable to resist the great wealth of reassurance streaming out towards her, she stood on tiptoe to rest her cheek momentarily against her father-in-law's.

He had accepted her without query or reserve. Not only did she have a family of her own at last—she was even an aunt!

Gregorio Fortunato spoke a trifle gruffly as he stepped back from her artless embrace to address his son.

'Serena and I must get back to our guests. It goes without saying you will be staying at the *fazenda* for a while. I'll leave your mother to arrange the preparation of a room for you, and in the meantime,' he smiled, 'the band is playing, the food is being served. I can only repeat what I said to everyone earlier—the night is young—enjoy yourselves!'

'Oh, Vitor, I don't think I've ever been happier in my whole life!' Her whole body glowing from the exhilaration of dancing in his arms, her hair a cloud of pale gold framing her heart-shaped face, it was several hours later that Ria allowed herself to be led over to one of many small tables scattered round the perimeter of the dance-area. 'I wish this night would last for ever!'

'Do you indeed?' Vitor spoke with assumed reproach. 'You forget I'm older than you. I'm not sure my bones can stand all this activity.'

'You have beautiful bones,' she responded dreamily. 'And you're only just thirty, Vitor, why, you haven't even reached your prime yet!'

'Thank you, *meu amor*, for the testimonial,' he retorted drily. 'For a child you're very perceptive.' His mouth curled in a mocking smile, and suddenly Ria's happiness drained away, leaving her feeling empty and isolated.

'I'm not a child,' she flared back hotly, the blood flaming her face as she recalled the consequences following her last angry assertion of the same fact. In her annoyance she refused to occupy the chair he was holding out for her.

'Are you not, *meu amor*?' It was a quizzical look Vitor offered her as he nodded down towards the waiting chair. 'If that's the truth, then it's one I prefer not to acknowledge. Now, sit down, please. Because even if you can dance all night without stopping, I feel very much in need of some refreshment.'

Ria's mouth closed mutinously, but she did as she was bid, subsiding with natural grace, her eyes following the tall figure of her husband as he made his way through the groups of guests to the bar and buffet.

Why couldn't he see she wasn't the child he insisted on calling her? Ria bit her lips in chagrin. The truth was she was a woman matured beyond her years. Not only had she had her first-hand experience of the seamier side of life during her years in the squalor of the *favela*, despite the loving protection of her mother which had acted as a buffer between herself and the most evil manifestations, but she had willingly assumed the responsibility of contributing to the meagre family budget by toiling in the car-parks of the big stores acting as an unofficial porter for a few *centavos* a day. And all this, she thought with uncharacteristic bitterness, at an age when her more fortunate contemporaries had nothing more on their minds than the colour of their next party dress!

Thoughtfully she extended her left hand in front of her, moving it gently so that the overhead lights caught the facets of the emerald, eliciting from it a shaft of scintillating green fire. How magnificent it was. A soft self-mocking laugh escaped her lips—and she had thought it was glass! Perhaps in some things she was naïve. First poverty and then seclusion had denied her experience of things that other girls of her age, born into the society of which she had now become a part, took for granted, had even grown bored with. Perhaps her unstinted enjoyment and enthusiasm did appear childlike to someone of Vitor's sophistication—if so, they were deceptive. She possessed a woman's heart and a woman's body—and she was capable of a woman's devoted, enduring love for the man of her choice.

*   *   *

To her unspoken disappointment Vitor didn't lead her on to the dance-floor again; instead he made a point of walking around with her, introducing her personally to all his friends and acquaintances.

She was thrilled with the reception she was given; even Felicia bestowed a smile on her although her whispered, 'I admire you so much, being prepared to take over Marta's role. I hope it won't prove too dispiriting for you,' could have been more tactfully phrased. Although, Ria allowed drily, congratulating herself on her newly discovered acumen, it had never been Felicia's intention to be tactful rather than hurtful!

Had the other girl really expected Vitor to go back to her after Marta's death? If so, it had been a grave misjudgement on her part. Ria herself had only known him for a comparatively short time, but she understood enough of his character to realise that his decisions were indomitable. Unless, of course, Vitor hadn't confessed the truth to her when he said he had never cared for Felicia.

Exchanging handshakes with yet another couple, Ria silently acknowledged herself relieved that Gustavo Veloso had left. She could admit honestly now what she had striven to repress for so long. She had never liked the man. It had been gratitude that had forced her to pretend she had, but she had always experienced an antipathy in his presence, an animal awareness of danger. Dear lord—what would her future have held if Vitor hadn't thrust himself into her life and rearranged it?

It was well past midnight when they parted from the last couple to whom she had been introduced and Vitor glanced down at the gold watch on his wrist.

'It's been a long day, Ria. Mama tells me our room has been prepared and I suggest we make a move to retire for the night.' He looked around. 'As you can see, others are beginning to leave now, and my parents will understand if we don't wait until everyone has gone.'

'As you wish, Vitor.' Ria bowed to his wishes, sensing he was in no mood to be opposed. It would have been nice to have been asked if she was ready to leave the party while it was still in process, she thought a trifle truculently. It was all very well telling her his parents would understand their early withdrawal. What he meant was his parents would put their own interpretation on their son and his bride of a few weeks choosing to have an early night!

As she allowed Vitor to lead her into the house she stole a look at his set profile. Did he in fact mean to suggest to her in private that they should reconsider their previous arrangement? A wild pulse started beating in her throat as reaching their room he stood aside to allow her to enter.

It was an enormous room, its wide balcony fronting the extensive gardens surrounding the house, its centre dominated by an ivory satin-covered double bed. Fitted furniture around the perimeter of the room supplied ample storage space while leaving a large area of pale blue carpet available for two free-standing comfortable-looking armchairs.

In one corner was a door, presumably leading to a bathroom, Ria surmised. The fact was confirmed when Vitor suggested she should have first use of it, before walking out on to the balcony to stand staring down at the thinning crowd of guests beneath him.

Efficiently she unpacked the small case Vitor had insisted she bring with her, and going into the bathroom showered before putting on the nightdress and negligée that had been his first gift to her.

Minutes later, her face devoid of make-up, her hair brushed and shining round her pale face, she walked out to join Vitor on the balcony. Sliding her arms round his waist in the darkness, she felt his instinctive reaction to her touch as his whole body tensed.

Embarrassed and hurt by the covert rejection, she hastily withdrew her tentative caress, swallowing the lump in her throat to say evenly, 'I just came out to let you know the bathroom's free.'

'Thank you.' The words echoed after her as she turned on her heel, re-entered the bedroom and slipped between the sheets.

'Goodnight, *menina*.' His shadow loomed over her. 'Your troubles are well behind you now. Sleep well.' He bent to kiss her cheek, a chaste salute that was worse than nothing, since she had been made to endure the fleeting torment of his nearness—only to have it removed from her in seconds.

'Goodnight,' she mumbled ungraciously, aping a weariness she didn't feel. *Menina* indeed! His habit of calling her 'child' was infuriating. As he well knew, many Brazilian girls of her age were married with children. Just because she had an English father didn't mean she was any less mature than her Brazilian half-sisters. Somehow she was going to have to find a way of proving that fact to Vitor. And when she had convinced him, she must try to win his affection, since it seemed his love was not attainable.

She turned on her other side, burying her head in the pillow, trying to ignore the sound of the bathroom shower and the picture of Vitor stripped and beautiful that it brought to her mind. What chance did she really stand, compared with the vital, clever Marta whom Vitor had left home for, and the lovely, elegant Felicia, who, despite turning Vitor down, had been one of the first to welcome him back?

The days that followed did nothing to restore her confidence. Vitor acted as her friend, mentor and guide, showing her round the estate, treating her with a fond tolerance in public and what seemed to her to be a cool forbearance when they were alone.

Only in the daytime when they were joined by Ricardo, who had continued to stay at the *fazenda*, did Ria find herself relaxing and enjoying herself.

She spent some time with Serena, finding a natural affinity with Vitor's mother, who introduced her into the art of running the *fazenda* efficiently from a domestic viewpoint, although, since they were amply staffed with servants, she wasn't allowed to do anything practical.

'Consider, my dear,' the older woman had told her gently. 'These girls rely on us for their wages. Should they find we're performing some of their tasks they'll be afraid they're going to be dismissed. Several have young children to support, and since the recession many of their husbands have no work of their own.'

It was a valid argument and one which Ria from experience was more than willing to acknowledge, although it left her with a great deal of time on her hands.

They had been at the *fazenda* for just over a week when Vitor announced one day after lunch that he and Ricardo were going to ride the boundaries of the estate at the expressed wish of Gregorio.

'If one renegade can force his way in, who knows how many others may succeed?' he asked mockingly, before his dark eyes turned to look at Ria. 'I'd invite you to accompany us but I seem to recall that the last time you were astride a horse you found the experience unpleasant.' His smile was little short of malicious.

'Extremely unpleasant,' she retorted with a sharp lift of her pert chin. 'And who better than you to know why?'

He laughed, reaching out to encircle her waist, giving her an intimate squeeze. 'One day I shall teach you to ride, *menina*, but for the present you will forgive me for deserting you, *não*?'

'Of course,' she answered him sweetly. 'I shall take the opportunity of sitting in the garden and doing some reading.'

She watched the two young men leave the stable yard, marvelling at their graceful strength as they steered their mounts southwards, before going into the well stocked library maintained by her father-in-law to find something to her taste.

It was two hours later when, bored with reading, she decided to take a stroll. She had wandered about half a mile down the perimeter road when she heard the sound of childish voices and realised she was walking in the direction of the school. Of course, how stupid of her! It was one of the first places Vitor had shown her and she had decided at the time to pay it a return visit. How could she have forgotten?

Obviously lessons had finished for the day when she entered the specially constructed playground, but there were still many children around playing on the equipment. Immediately she was surrounded. Delighted by her welcome, she was only too pleased to join in their games, her slender body fitting easily into the swings and sections of the roundabout, even counterbalancing two of the youngest children on the see-saw. She was laughingly refusing to attempt the slide, afraid this was one piece of apparatus which hadn't been designed to accommodate her shapely feminine hips, when she heard a woman's voice break through the high-pitched childish tones surrounding her.

'Senhora Fortunato, what a pleasure to see you again.'

Startled Ria turned her head. Had her mother-in-law followed her? Instead of Serena Fortunato she found herself meeting the smiling gaze of Amelia Rodrigues, the schoolteacher. An embarrassed blush rose in her face as she realised the mistake she had made.

'Forgive me,' she said with a wry smile. 'I haven't got used to being called by my married name. I'd far rather you called me Ria.'

'Of course, if you wish it.' Amelia Rodrigues was in her mid-thirties, a good-looking woman whose husband helped in the administration of the *fazenda*. 'It would be my pleasure to offer you some refreshment. If you came here on foot you must be feeling thirsty.'

'That would be lovely.' Happily Ria accepted the invitation. If she and Vitor were to stay at the *fazenda* for any length of time, perhaps this would be something to occupy her. Surely she could do something useful, if it was only hearing the children read, or supervising them in the playground? Since it was Gregorio who was providing the facility she would have to have his permission, and of course Vitor would have to be consulted, she supposed, but first she must see if Amelia would approve the idea.

It was a further two hours before she left, refusing with gratitude Amelia's invitation to join her and her family for their evening meal.

Walking back through the playground, she was jubilant. Not only had the schoolteacher welcomed her suggestion, but she felt she had made a real friend of the other woman. It was incredible how quickly the time had passed. Fortunately the evening meal at the *fazenda* wasn't until eight o'clock, which meant she still had more than enough time to get back and change.

The small playground was deserted now, the children indoors preparing for their dinner. Passing the roundabout, Ria gave it a push. Still deep in thought she paused at the swings, then impulsively seated herself on one using her arms and legs to send it flying higher and higher, enjoying the sense of freedom and power as she soared through the air. If only she could escape from her own problems with such ease! Still, she had achieved something. If she was to be denied her own children she would enjoy other people's. It would be a poor compensation but at least it would be something!

'I might have guessed I'd find you here, *menina*!' There was no mistaking the exasperation in Vitor's tone as his words broke through her meditation. Or the contempt in his epithet. 'What the hell do you think you're playing at—disappearing without telling anyone where you were going? My mother's been half out of her mind with worry! Get down here, Ria!'

'There's no need to speak to me like that!' she called down to him haughtily. The fact he had some reason on his side did nothing to reduce her angry reaction to his harsh instructions, but she did use her body and legs to break her speed. 'I'd have been back in plenty of time for dinner,' she justified herself trenchantly.

'Would you indeed,' he declared pitilessly, moving behind her to grab at the swing in mid-arc before it stopped. Unprepared for the interference her grip on the chains wasn't strong enough to prevent her from sliding off the seat to land in a heap on the ground, where she lay, her heart thumping with fright and rage, shaken but uninjured.

'How dare you?' she flung at him furiously as he walked round to stare at her recumbent figure on the ground at his feet. 'You've hurt me!'

'Only your pride,' Vitor offered callously. 'The rubber landing-mat beneath you was designed to protect silly children who lost control of themselves.'

'I didn't lose control. You deliberately made me fall off—and I weigh a lot more than a child. It was a heavy landing!' She stretched the truth, actually shaking with fury and having to suppress a violent urge to attack the arrogant man before her who had engineered her humiliating downfall.

'It would have been much heavier if the chains had broken and you'd landed away from the mats on the concrete,' Vitor asserted with cruel deliberation. 'The structure is regularly tested but it's intended for lightweights.' There was a barbaric gleam in his eyes as he pulled her roughly to her feet and let his eyes wander over her body. 'However much of a child you are at heart, you weigh a deal more than a ten-year-old. Don't tell me you didn't know you were taking the structure to its limits and daring disaster with that bravado display?'

Very well, if he wasn't going to believe her protestations she would stay silent. Ria clamped her lips shut, feeling a vibrant electricity building up between them, and knowing if she didn't keep a rein on her temper she would say things she might live to regret.

Vitor scowled down at her mutinous face before pushing his fingers through his hair and giving an exaggerated sigh. 'Didn't you even realise that when you couldn't be found anywhere in the house or garden the alarm might be raised? Apart from the potentially dangerous circumstances surrounding our marriage, you're still a stranger to the area. You could have wandered away and got lost, or worse still been injured or even killed without our knowing where to look for you!'

He paused, obviously expecting a sign of her repentance. Prepared to admit she had been a little thoughtless, Ria still resented his arbitrary condemnation. He could keep her standing here all night unless she knuckled down to his authority and gave him the apology he saw as his due though, and she was beginning to feel the pangs of hunger.

'I'm sorry for any inconvenience I caused,' she told him stiffly. 'As I told you before, I always meant to return in good time for dinner. If I gave your mother cause for concern then I regret that too, and will tell her so as soon as I see her.'

'Yes, indeed you will.' He took hold of her arm with ungentle fingers. 'It was fortunate I returned sooner than expected. My father contacted me by short-wave radio to let me know a business acquaintance of his will be dining with us tonight. He's heard of my return and is interested in letting my new partnership handle all his legal affairs. By the time I'd returned your absence had been noticed and the entire household was in chaos.'

Ria allowed herself to be led to where the estate's Range Rover stood. Taking the seat beside Vitor, she clamped her mouth into a hard line lest she should give way to the tears which threatened her.

Vitor was over-reacting, making her appear irresponsible and discourteous, neither of which adjectives she deserved. Now was certainly not the time to broach the subject of spending some time at the estate school. Perhaps later, when her imperious husband had been sweetened by the promised business deal, she might venture the subject. Until then she would stay silent and hope his fury would burn itself out before she was obliged to accompany him to dinner.

She kept her resolve while Vitor informed the *fazenda* by radio that she had been found safe and well and he was returning with her. Like so much lost luggage, she thought rebelliously, affronted by his terse tone. She sighed, turning to gaze out of the window as the car gathered speed. Of course, by eluding his jurisdiction she had disputed his right of authority over her. In male-dominated Brazil that seeming act of defiance was tantamount to slapping his face!

As if augmenting her conclusion, Vitor drove the vehicle with a ferocious skill. Hanging grimly to the seat, Ria bit back the angry words that would have condemned him as reckless. It would have been pointless to tell him she had felt safer on the swing than sitting beside him when he was in this black mood.

Reminding herself that discretion was the better part of valour, she maintained her stony silence as Vitor accompanied her up the stairs to their room.

'You have half an hour to make yourself respectable,' he directed harshly. 'Since time is so short I shall avail myself of the bathroom in my parents' room as they've already finished their toilette and are ready to meet our guests.'

'Guests?' Ria found her voice. 'There is more than one expected?'

'Yes, we shall be nine at table,' Vitor tendered briefly. 'So I'd be obliged if you would wear something formal. Apart from the family, Felicia and her parents are joining us as well as Senhor Olvidades. Since the latter is something of a celebrity in São Paolo, being one of its chief industrialists, his legal affairs could bring me in excellent business. It would please me if you could make a good impression on your first meeting with him. Do I make myself clear?' A dark eyebrow rose as his hostile gaze traversed her ruffled appearance.

'Heitor Olvidades?' A shocking pain was convulsing her, twisting a knife into her heart, strangling her vocal cords. 'I can't dine with *him*, Vitor...I can't!'

CHAPTER ELEVEN

'DON'T be absurd,' Vitor snapped irritably. 'There's no need to let his standing in society disquiet you.' He walked away from her, sliding the wardrobe door open to take out his clothes for the evening. 'With a little care you'll be able to make yourself as presentable as Felicia, I'm sure. If you find yourself unable to converse intelligently, then confine yourself to listening and smiling prettily. Olvidades is a lonely man, a widower without issue. He'll no doubt fine your youthful freshness quite charming.'

At any other time his casual dismissal of her abilities would have stung an angry rebuttal from her, now she had more important things to consider.

'I won't do it, Vitor, I can't!' She seized his arm as he went to brush past her. 'You don't understand.'

'Oh, yes, I do!' He flung his clothes down on the bed, taking her by the arms, his fingers digging into her soft flesh. 'You're cross and ill-tempered because I took you to task for disrupting the household, and this is your idea of taking revenge—making me look a fool by refusing to take your place at my side at a social gathering which could have far reaching effects on my future.'

'I could make you look a bigger fool should I agree to what you're asking,' she mumbled under her breath, taken aback by the strength of the antagonism directed at her.

'So that's the way the land lies, is it?' Ria quailed from the soft menace of Vitor's reply. 'I can see the lesson you've just been taught hasn't had the necessary salutary effect. Let me warn you there are plenty more available from the same book which could affect you more painfully!'

'Thrash me then!' Ria taunted emotively, her breast heaving with an angry passion. 'You—you bully. See if I care!'

'Oh, you'd care, *querida*,' he informed her huskily. 'But that's not my intention at the moment—although since you invite it, I'll keep the option open. For the time being all I intend to do is remind you, you are my wife, and within the limited terms of our marriage I expect a degree of obedience from you.'

Before Ria realised his intention he had swung her round in his arms and taken her lips with a brutal indifference. She could feel him trembling with a controlled emotion as he moulded her body against his own, pushing her backwards so that she had no choice but to raise her arms and cling to him for support lest she should fall.

She was still gasping for breath as his mouth released her to travel down her throat, finding its way to where her breast swelled above the satin and lace supporting it. Burning streams of fire flowed through her veins, every nerve in her body tensed and trembled as he nuzzled her soft flesh with an innate delicacy.

'Vitor...' She breathed his name, the sound welling up from the deep agony within her. What he was doing was a travesty of what she wanted so desperately from him!

'*Mai de Deus,* Ria!' He released her with a suddenness that left her reeling. Stopping only to repossess the discarded clothes, he made for the door, turning on the threshold to repeat his instructions.

'Half an hour, Ria—a little less now. Forget whatever you were. Remember who you are now and try to behave accordingly or you will have me to answer to later.'

She made the deadline with seconds to spare and hesitated on the threshold of the salon. Forget who she was, her overbearing husband had instructed her. Oh, if only she could! Vitor was determined she shouldn't shame him by her absence. With her hand on the door she prayed for the strength not to shame him by her presence.

The pleasant murmur of voices stopped as she entered and every eye turned to regard her. They were all there as Vitor had said. Felicia dramatically beautiful in a floor-length gown of black and white striped silk; her parents elegant in their formal clothes; Serena as lovely as ever in midnight blue; the other men immaculate in dark evening trousers and light jackets.

Tonight was a special night in more ways than one and Ria had dressed for it accordingly. Among the clothes Vitor had provided for her was an evening gown of such breathtaking sophistication she had never imagined herself wearing it in public. Because it was the epitome of everything in life she had never expected to possess she had brought it with her to the *fazenda*, loath to leave it unguarded at the apartment. Child indeed! Vitor's contempt had spurred her to select it for the evening. She would show him and everyone else there she was no child!

The pale ice-blue velvet was strapless, lying low across her breasts so that their perfect pale cleavage was shown to its stunning advantage. From there it sculpted her slender curves with awesome fidelity so that any fault in the symmetry of her form would not escape detection. There was none. From the opaline sheen of her creamy shoulders to the almond toe of her matching shoes beneath the straight sweep of skirt she was perfect. Every eye turned to her registered it.

Blonde hair swept upwards, caught at the crown in a tumble of curls, served to draw attention to the flawless lines of her face. Lashes and brows dramatically darkened, cheeks flushed with trepidation, lips pencilled and brushed to a velvet purity before the application of the gloss which bedewed them, Ria surveyed the other guests, her head held regally high, conscious of the fact she wore a small fortune in diamonds suspended in a falling cluster from each small ear. Apart from these glistening chandeliers, the only other jewellery she wore was her wedding-ring.

'I'm sorry if I kept everyone waiting.' With a great effort she modulated her voice, keeping it low and husky. She was a little later than she had intended, having come face to face with Serena outside her bedroom door. It was then her mother-in-law had insisted on her wearing the diamonds. 'I never wear them now, my dear. They need a young girl's neck to show them to advantage. You'd be doing me a favour by letting them see the light.'

At first Ria had demurred, then, seeing the offer was sincerely meant, she had accepted it with gratitude, returning to her own room to place them comfortably while Serena returned to the company she had just left.

'You know everyone here except Senhor Olvidades.' It was Vitor who came forward, a deep glow of satisfaction gleaming in his dark eyes at the vision she made. Ria's heart beat with a throbbing, almost painful rhythm, sending the blood singing in her ears as she felt his hand tremble slightly beneath her elbow.

She had massaged every inch of her skin with Balmain's Ivoire body cream, so she was surrounded by a subtle evocative fragrance as she permitted Vitor to lead her across the room to where Heitor Olvidades had risen to greet her.

He was as she had always imagined. Just as her mother had described him. A powerfully built man in his mid-sixties, handsome as a fighting bull. Strong and proud, stubborn and unbending. A man respected and admired in industrial cities not only in São Paolo but all over Brazil. If he was going to pass over his legal affairs to Vitor it would be a magnificent acquisition for the younger man, instantly giving him the credibility he needed to launch out on the new career in politics he envisaged.

It was a meeting she had never wanted, but for Vitor's sake she must pretend. Swallowing deeply, fighting down her repulsion, Ria extended her hand and allowed it to lie quiescent in that of of her maternal grandfather.

'I'm delighted to meet your acquaintance, *senhora*.' The greeting he gave her was formal, his voice deep and resonant as he lifted her hand and brushed the back against his lips.

'*Senhor*.' She was cool and distant, every nerve of her body straining to control the shudder of distaste that threatened to convulse her, glad when she felt Vitor's hand rest lightly on her waist to turn her towards the dining-room as the meal's readiness was announced.

The conversation was spirited and general, the food delicious and the wine flowed. Ria sat outwardly demure, inwardly seething, turning her lovely head to follow the conversation, smiling and nodding to show her interest but contributing nothing.

At the head of the table, the guest of honour, sat the man who had been the instrument of his own daughter's appalling, unnecessary death. Inside her a little voice prompted her she should judge not lest she herself be judged. Angrily she ignored it. She wasn't without sin, and she was prepared to answer for her faults at the day of judgement, but she would never turn from her door anyone who needed her help—especially someone she purported to love.

She lifted the edge of her hand to her eyes to obliterate the furious tears that had sprung from them, and caught Vitor's worried gaze from across the table.

'What is it, Ria?' There was no disguising his anxiety as his deep soft voice reached her beneath the higher-pitched level of general conversation. 'Dear God—did I really hurt you earlier this evening?' He was pale beneath his golden tan. 'Do you need a doctor, Ria—are you in pain, *querida*? You've hardly eaten a mouthful.' He made a move to push his chair away from the table.

'Vitor, please, I'm fine,' she lied bravely. 'I swear to you I'm not in pain!' Only in my heart, she wept inwardly, and that agony is none of your making.

He continued looking at her, his eyes dark pools of unhappiness, his jaw taut with strain. A great rush of love for him overwhelmed her. If only she could take him away from the table and express what she felt for him, convince him she was trying to be the wife he needed—even if she wasn't the one he really wanted.

'Honestly,' she assured him. 'There's nothing the matter with me. It's just I prefer to listen rather than talk.' To prove her sincerity she forced herself to take another spoonful of the meringue and cream dessert before her. It was tasteless in her mouth, already corrupted by the bitterness in her heart, but she swallowed it and smiled reassuringly across the table.

She had sworn she would never stay in the same room as the man who had destroyed her mother, let alone sit at the same table or touch his hand in greeting, but for Vitor's sake she would see the evening through. In a few hours her ordeal would be over.

What she hadn't anticipated was the turn the conversation would take. Arising ironically from her own interest in the local school, warmly attested to by Ricardo who had accompanied her and Vitor on her first visit, the talk swung naturally to families. Who asked the question she could never afterwards remember. It was Heitor Olvidades's answer which rang loud and clear down the table towards her.

'No, unfortunately, I have no children. My only daughter died young.'

It was too much. The sound of Ria's crystal wineglass falling to the polished wood floor overrode the murmur of polite regret that followed his sanctimonious pronouncement as she sprang to her feet, her self-control shattered to shreds.

Eyes flared in furious brilliance down the length of the table; her voice was as cold and cutting as a steel blade as Ria addressed the perpetrator of what he supposed to be a lie.

'Really, *senhor*? I'm surprised you're aware of the fact, since her pauper's grave has been unmarked by flowers since the day death released her from the foul agony of typhoid!' She heard the gasp of shock that echoed round the table, but she had gone too far to retract. Glaring haughtily at the astounded face of her grandfather she added cuttingly, 'But perhaps you find the streets of the *favela* too unsavoury for your taste—although they were all your daughter and her baby knew from the day you shut your door on them!'

'Caterina died nearly twenty years ago the day she defied and disgraced me!' Olvidades was on his feet facing her, his face paper-white, his jaw so tightly clenched she could see the muscles of his cheek bunching in protest.

'Caterina died six years ago in a rat-infested, disease-ridden hovel—I should know because I was at her side!'

Tears were streaming down her face as she re-lived the pain of those past years, the agony of a child deprived of the only love she knew. Large glistening tears fell down her pale face leaving it unmarked, their only evidence the shimmering sparkling beauty of her wide eyes as she confronted the man she held responsible for her grief.

'Who are you?' Olvidades gripped the edge of the table, as a grey tinge entered his face.

Completely unaware of the silent stunned audience around them, Ria sucked in a hard breath. He knew who she was. He just wanted her to confirm it, and it was her pleasure to do so.

'I'm Caterina's daughter,' she told him. Straight and beautiful, head held high she dared anyone present to condemn her. 'I resemble my father, but I have the misfortune to carry some of your blood in my veins, *senhor*!' Blindly she reached on the table, found what she was seeking and lifted the knife to her wrist. 'Believe me, nothing would give me greater pleasure than ridding my body of its taint for ever!'

The block of ice that had frozen her was melting now as she felt the blade against her skin. Oh, God in heaven, what had she done! Now she could hear the unnatural silence in the room, see the shocked surprise and pity on the faces of Ricardo and Serena, the smug curiosity on Felicia's countenance.

It was enough! She dared not search out her husband's response to her outburst. The horror of what she had done was only just beginning to seep through into her consciousness. Someone spoke her name, but she didn't wait to find out who. Letting the knife slip from her nerveless hand, she fled from the room.

In the sanctuary of her bedroom she knew only the need to escape, to run from the disgrace she had brought upon herself. She cared nothing for the shocked angry face of Olvidades, but to have abused the hospitality of Vitor's parents whom she had grown to love and to mortify Vitor in front of his friends and family, to destroy his prospects, were unforgivable sins. She had no idea where she could go, but there would be somewhere. There was always somewhere...

Her breath coming in great gasps of despair, she struggled with the zip-fastener of her dress, sobbing her distress as it remained stubbornly in place beneath her urgent fingers. At last it gave and she was able to step from the dress, tossing it down on the bed, her trembling fingers rising to her ears. Dear heavens, she had nearly forgotten the earrings. To leave them still in place would brand her a thief.

The tiny gold screws were fiddly to undo and she had only just managed to release them when the door to the room was flung open and Vitor appeared on the threshold.

Dressed only in the flesh-coloured body stocking that fitted her like a second skin, Ria cowered away from his angry presence, her hands rising instinctively to cover herself from his inflammatory gaze.

'For the love of God, Ria, why didn't you confide in me—tell me who he was?'

He had kicked the door shut behind him and stood glaring at her, his voice throbbing with emotion, his hands clenched at his sides.

'I—I tried to,' she whispered, the words dry and cracked as they issued from her parched throat.

'So you did.' He swallowed deeply. 'And I wasn't in the mood to listen. How in hell could I have imagined such a thing happening! I didn't even realise you knew your maternal grandfather's name!'

'My mother told me. Although she refused to bear it, she did tell me who he was and how he rejected us both—not once, but twice.' Locked in her grief the words came spilling out. 'When my mother first left his house she was lucky enough to get a job as a lady's maid to an old lady who was very kind to her, saw her through her pregnancy and allowed her to keep me with her. Then when I was about four, she died.'

'Go on,' Vitor instructed tersely. 'Then what happened?'

It was impossible to judge the degree of his anger, but from the tough line of his jaw and the dark fury of his lustrous eyes, Ria could take no comfort. But his command left her no alternative but to obey, although all she really wanted to do was to be alone with her ignominy.

'After her death we had nowhere to go. Mama managed to get a couple of temporary jobs, but she had no skills and maids were easy to get and easy to discharge.' Her voice sank to a whisper. 'That's when we started to live in the *favela*. After a while, when things were really bleak, she got the job in the Veloso household—only of course at the time I didn't know where it was—and things got better. She bought me some shoes and I went to school and then—you know what happened.'

'Yes.' Vitor's bleak monosyllable confirmed his awareness.

Ria's fingers bit into her palms in her distress. 'She was desperate. She'd always hoped my father would return. If he'd gone to her father's house there were servants there who knew where to find her and they would've told him. But by then she was beginning to believe he must be injured or dead.'

'Or had simply deserted her?' Vitor suggested with compassion.

'No. She loved him, you see. She never believed that, but she was unable to prove anything. All she knew about him was he was engaged on highly confidential work for the British government—something scientific in the Antarctic. Their time together had been so short. When they parted she hadn't even realised she was carrying me, and she couldn't remember any of the details he'd told her about his family in England.'

'Poor little girl.' Sympathy deepened Vitor's voice. 'She couldn't have been much older than you are now.'

'Not much, no. That was when she went back to her father, swallowed her pride for my sake, begged him to take me in even if he couldn't forgive her. He—he just walked away from her. Summoned one of the servants to show her out of the house.'

Unable to meet the ferocity of Vitor's hard face, Ria looked away, her whole slender frame heaving with a terrible grief. 'For years I've hated him, carried the sin of being unable to absolve him like a black stain on my soul. But my mother...' Her voice broke uncontrollably. 'Mama forgave him before she died. I know she would want me to do the same but until tonight I never even wanted to set eyes on him...and then, when I saw him...after a while something very strange happened. I wanted a miracle.'

She paused, her eyes fastened to Vitor's strained face, seeing the harsh lines that marred it, the stern thrust of the clenched jaw. He looked as if he could murder her, but she was beyond fear, in a limbo of her own making, spilling out her forlorn hopes, her broken dreams, exposing the rawness of her spirit to the only man she had ever loved; confessing before him what she had only just admitted to herself.

'I prayed he'd become your client, that we should get to know him, that he would come to like me for myself—admire me even, because I was your wife, well dressed, well mannered . . . and that one day I would tell him who I was and he—he would take me in his arms and hold me—call me "granddaughter", tell me how much he regretted the past. Even swear that he'd tried to find Mama, employed enquiry agents to try and trace us—but to no avail . . .'

'*Mai de Deus*, Ria . . .' Vitor took a step towards her, a dark fire blazing from his eyes.

Clenching her hands against her heart as if their presence could quieten its furious pounding, she refused to stop her bitter self-castigation. 'And then he denied Mama's existence in front of everybody there. I looked at his face and there was no love or pity. No charity. And I saw myself for the fool I was. The stupid, romantic child you always knew me to be.'

Her voice thickened, became almost slurred with the weight of her anguish. 'I wanted to belong you see, Vitor. I wanted to have roots—to be someone in my own right, acknowledged as such. And then he said those cruel words and I knew I was living in a fool's paradise; that there are no such things as miracles.'

'No, Ria, that's not true.' Vitor's interception was oddly gentle in contrast to the bleakness of his expression. 'For the pure in heart there will always be miracles. Never lose your faith in them, *meu amor*, just because this time your prayer wasn't answered in the way you wanted it.'

His kindness, when she had expected—and deserved—abuse and scorn brought her to a stunned silence. Somehow she had to apologise for what she had done, the public scene she had created, and let him know she was going to make instant and complete reparation by removing her unwanted presence from his life.

'I can't ever repair the damage I've done tonight,' she whispered, barely audibly. 'But when I've gone the gossip will die down. In time it will be forgotten.'

'So you're running away, are you?' he rasped. 'That's why you're in such a state of undress, is it?' For the first time Ria saw a glimmer of amusement on his face, but the pain was still there, mirrored in his sable eyes and the grimness of his tight mouth. 'For a moment I thought you intended to use your charms to buy my forgiveness.'

Ria couldn't smile, her agony was too deeply rooted. 'I could never hope for your forgiveness,' she told him dully. 'Senhor Olvidades will never give you his business now.'

'On the contrary, Ria,' he moved across the room, taking her hands from her breasts and holding them in his own, 'I would never take his business. I've no use for inflexible tyrants. And as for my forgiveness—well, that's easily earned. Put on your dress and return downstairs. Olvidades made his excuses and left. However, our other guests remain and must be entertained. Your presence is necessary.'

'Vitor! I can't!' Horror manifested itself on her lovely tear-stained face even while she registered the fact that Vitor wasn't nearly as angry with her as she had feared—as she had deserved. 'I can't possibly face them again.'

'You can, you must—and you will!' His tone was implacable. 'You've nothing to be ashamed of. Olvidades has crept away, but you, *meu amor*, will not be allowed to follow his cowardly example. Be assured my parents have every sympathy with you and when they learn the whole story it will only serve to solidify their support. So, *namorada*, you will replace your dress and the earrings my mother has given you as a token of her real affection, and come downstairs with me.'

'Vitor, I can't, anything but that!' Piteously her large blue eyes implored him. 'I feel so humiliated. I can't face them.'

'Mai de Deus!' The oath exploded violently from relentless lips. 'Every minute you delay you're making it harder on yourself.' Before her puzzled regard his mouth split into a wolfish grin. 'But since you're being stubborn, allow me to assist you.'

Before the meaning of the words had penetrated her dazed mind Ria found one hand seized while his other arm thrust between her legs to lift her easily across his shoulder. Four strides and he was at the door.

'If you won't come voluntarily, then you shall do so involuntarily and just as you are at the moment.' His hand reached for the door knob.

'Put me down! Vitor!' Shock had penetrated through her haze of self-pity as Ria thumped her fists hard against his light jacket. 'Don't you dare, you...you...you *bandeirante*!'

'That's more like it, *querida*!' he said, laughing into her outraged face as he deposited her gently on the bed. 'I began to believe you'd lost your spirit; now I see it was only dormant.' He left her to stride across to the mirror and regard his own reflection. *'Bandeirante*, eh? Should I be insulted to be nominated as one of the brave and fierce fighters who opened up Brazil?'

Her battle lost, Ria rose from the bed and reached for her dress. 'They were also renowned as being violent, rapacious and cruel,' she informed him with a toss of her head. Beneath her newly found composure a wild joy was growing. Vitor had not disowned her, he was standing by her, demonstrating his faith in her.

'That's better,' he approved, moving towards her to draw up the zip fastener and watching while she replaced the earrings.

A few seconds to repair her make-up and she was ready for her ordeal.

At the door to the salon he paused to drop a light kiss on her forehead. '*Bandeirante*, hmm?' he mused thoughtfully. 'Well, we shall see.'

Three hours later as Felicia and her parents left, Ria had to admit the rest of the evening hadn't been the disaster she had anticipated. Her reappearance had been greeted with no more comment than if she had merely left the room to repair her make-up.

What had passed in her absence she hardly dared contemplate, but whatever had been said, it seemed she wasn't to be treated as the outcast she had felt herself to be.

Reaching their bedroom after bidding goodnight to her in-laws and Ricardo, Ria opened the balcony doors and stepped outside, inhaling the sweet night air.

Impulsively she turned to Vitor as she heard his step beside her. If he could forgive her for the scene she had made, wasn't there the smallest possible chance he had some feeling for her? If only she could spend the night in his arms instead of sleeping with her back turned to him, afraid to encroach on his body-space. Hesitantly her hands rose to his shoulders. 'Vitor...'

'Ria.' Firm competent hands took hers, removing them from his body, holding them. 'Tomorrow I have to go back to São Paolo. I've neglected the partnership I've entered into for far too long, and there are other important issues I have to attend to.'

'Yes, of course, I understand.' She smiled her content at him. Of course she would miss the *fazenda* and the opportunity to help out at the school, but her future lay

with Vitor wherever he went and she could only antici-
pate with a mounting excitement the thrill of being alone
with him once more. 'What time are we leaving?'

'I'm leaving after breakfast, but I shall be going alone.'
His handclasp round her hand tightened as he heard her
sharp cry of protest. 'I want you to stay here. It's your
home now as much as it's mine. My parents regard you
with a very deep affection as I'm sure you must realise,
and my cousin has guaranteed he will watch over you
in my absence.'

So she was to be punished after all and in the most
hurtful way of all. Proudly Ria refused to show the extent
of the pain he had inflicted on her.

'How long will you be away?' she asked politely.

'I don't know.' The answer was abrupt as he released
her hands to walk away, leaving her standing there gazing
out into the darkness, her dreams crumbling to dust.

CHAPTER TWELVE

'HAVE you heard from Vitor lately?' Ricardo enquired pleasantly as he helped Ria to dismount from the gleaming back of the sorrel filly, before raising an imperious hand to a nearby stable-lad to collect and groom their mounts.

'He phoned me yesterday,' she answered brightly. 'He's very busy, but he hopes to come down here for the weekend. He's going to be very surprised when he discovers I can manage a quiet horse without disgracing myself.' She laughed, her face alive with the memory of that first meeting with her arrogant husband. The sideways glance she shot at her companion invited him to admit he knew the details of that encounter, but he didn't respond to the bait. Ria sighed. Perhaps after all he wasn't as deeply in Vitor's confidence as she had at first believed. But then who was?

Six weeks had passed since that traumatic dinner party after which Vitor had departed for the city. Then it had been summer. Now the autumn was well advanced, the green berries on the coffee-trees had turned into a bright red, signifying the time for harvest—the busiest time of the year when everyone on the plantation would lend a hand to assist the small army of itinerant workers who would also be engaged.

With the fertile trees bearing as many as two thousand berries apiece, each one having to be picked separately to avoid fermentation, there was going to be a great period of prolonged labour before the harvest was safely hulled, stored and dried. Afterwards, Ricardo had told her, the dried berries would be bagged according to size and taken to Santos, the nearest port, for shipment.

How much she had appreciated his company. Always correct and courteous, he had managed to become a close friend without once having overstepped the boundaries of propriety. His Isabella was going to be a lucky girl, Ria mused. Was she perhaps even now dreaming about the tall handsome Brazilian rancher who was destined to become her husband?

'I'm surprised you're able to be away from your own ranch for so long.' Following her own train of thought, Ria spoke her mind, watching with amusement as he tipped his broad brimmed stockman's hat over his eyes.

'Delegation, that's the answer,' he returned easily. 'Besides, I had strict instructions from Vitor to ensure you were happy here and to report back to him instantly if you were not. He felt you would hide your feelings from my uncle and aunt should they not be favourable, but that your reservations would be less with me.' He grinned at her.

'He asked you to spy on me?' Ria was taken aback and showed it.

'Hardly that.' Ricardo denied it quickly. 'Since my uncle and aunt are particularly busy at this time of the year, the way Vitor put it to me was that I should escort and protect you in his absence and maintain your happiness wherever possible.'

'Which you've accomplished admirably,' she confirmed wryly. 'But what an imposition to place on you.'

Ricardo denied her assertion with an emphatic shake of his head. 'When we were teenagers Vitor once saved me from being gored by a bull. I probably owe him my life, and after all what he requested of me was a pleasure, not a penance.' He swept her a stylish bow. 'And I've been very pleased to let your husband know you seem

very contented with your environment, that your relations with your in-laws are highly amicable, that, I,
myself, am enslaved by your grace and beauty but...'
he paused dramatically as his smile faded.

'But...' Ria prompted. 'But what?'

Ricardo raised a dark eyebrow as he met her puzzled
gaze. 'But that in my opinion he has neglected you long
enough, and it's hardly surprising that on many occasions when you believe yourself to be unobserved you
have an air of *tristesse* about you—and that since the
time has arrived when I must return to Rio Grande do
Sul to ride my own range and check up on my *gauchos*,
the time has also arrived when he should return to the
Fazenda Graciela and meet his own obligations as a
married man.'

'Oh, Ricardo, you didn't!' Her horror was echoed in
Ria's shaking voice.

Ricardo shrugged. 'It's no more than the truth, Ria.
If Vitor found it offensive, then retrospection will soften
his reaction to it. Despite present evidence, he's far from
the unfeeling brute he appears to be.'

Oh, dear heavens, this was going from bad to worse!
Vitor certainly wouldn't have been very pleased to receive such an admonishment from his younger cousin.
It had been a courageous and affectionate action for him
to take on her behalf, but decidedly ill-advised! No
wonder Vitor had advised her of his imminent return.

'You can't fool me, Ria.' There was a thread of anger
in Ricardo's normally pleasant light baritone. 'You've
been eating your heart out for him. You've lost weight,
and despite the fact that your pale skin has turned golden
from exposure to the sun, I've seen the vitality drain
from you over the past weeks.' He reached out and
grasped her shoulders in a firm hold, forcing her to look
him straight in the eyes.

'Vitor is my master in many things—but if he cannot see the pain he is causing you by spending all his time in São Paolo, then he must be told. *Meu Deus*—he's in love with you, Ria. I can't believe he's so stupid he can't see the damage he's doing!'

'Who's stupid? And what damage?'

Ricardo's hands dropped from Ria's shoulders as she turned wide-eyed and gasping to meet Vitor's cool enigmatic appraisal.

'You nearly frightened me to death!' She pressed the back of her hand to her heart, fighting to gain control of her shocked emotions as he continued to eye her impersonally, allowing his gaze to drift from the pale blue cotton shirt that clung to her heaving breasts, past the fitted heavy denim trousers that followed the slender line of her hip and thigh to the beautiful high leather boots she wore.

'I was able to get away sooner than I expected.' He glanced at Ricardo before returning his steady scrutiny to Ria. She could sense the cool chasm opening between the two men, knew she was somehow involved in their newly found antagonism, yet felt helpless to intervene.

'I asked you a question, Ria. Who's stupid—and what damage?'

It hadn't been she who had used the phrases, but clearly it was she who was going to supply the meaning. This was no time to be honest! Not with Ricardo's face set into a hard mask and Vitor glowering at them both as if he had caught them making love rather than returning from a perfectly innocuous ride through the estate.

Inspiration came to her. 'Ricardo was talking about one of the new stable-boys. He—he was breaking in a filly and he was—was too rough on her. Her mouth was cut.'

'A bad occurrence.' Vitor nodded gravely. 'You will give my father his name and the boy will be dismissed.' Cool dark eyes sought the other man's set face. 'Perhaps you could speak to the head groom about it for me, Rico.'

He received a curt nod as the other man recognised and accepted his dismissal.

Casting a quick look at Vitor's grim expression, Ria wished she could think of something to say to break the tension between them. She had longed for the day when she would see Vitor again, and now it seemed it was going to be a disaster. She could have wept.

It was Vitor who broke the silence between them as Ricardo's tall striding figure receded into the stable-yard.

'I've already called in at the house. Mama told me you'd gone out riding with Ricardo and would be returning shortly. I see his lessons have been successful.' A carelessly raised eyebrow invited her response.

'I thought you'd be pleased,' she returned in a small voice, seeing nothing on his stern face to justify her opinion. Didn't he realise she would far rather have had him teach her the skills of horsemanship than Ricardo—however skilled the latter's tuition had been?

'Of course I'm pleased you've found ways to amuse yourself. I understand you've made yourself a firm favourite with everyone here—including the children.'

Was there a hint of criticism in his smooth tone?

Hands on her hips, a trace of belligerence entered her reply.

'Everyone—your family, your friends and your employees—has gone out of his or her way to make me welcome. Your father's told me all about the life of a *fazeindera* and your mother has arranged for a dressmaker to provide me with a new wardrobe according to the request you made to her before you left.' Her head rose a little higher. 'And my social life has increased beyond belief. I've received so many invitations from your friends I was afraid I'd turn into a social butterfly, so since it isn't appropriate for me to help with the household chores I've been helping out at the school.' She stopped as she perceived the darkness of Vitor's brow. Good grief! Was nothing she had done going to meet with his approval?

'Your cousin Ricardo,' she added firmly, determined not to be cowed by his saturnine appraisal, 'has done everything in his means to instruct and amuse me in your absence. Apart from teaching me to ride, he's...'

'I'm delighted my cousin has taken such a close interest in your welfare!' Vitor broke across her sentence, the comment so nearly a snarl that Ria's eyes flashed indignantly.

'I thought that was his brief!'

'His "brief", as you call it, was to keep you away from danger in my absence. I couldn't entirely rule out the possibility that Veloso might attempt to contact you.'

'I could have come with you to São Paolo and stayed with you in the apartment—and you could have protected me yourself!' she snapped, furiously affronted by what she saw as his lack of reasonableness.

'So you could—if I'd thought I could trust you when my back was turned!'

'Oh!' Ria bit back the angry rebuttal that sprang to her tongue. They were quarrelling, when all she wanted to do was fling herself into Vitor's arms, feel the strength of his embrace, lift up her face and feel his mouth take her own.

Suddenly in the warmth of the autumn afternoon, Ria felt her body drenched in a cold sweat. Vitor had achieved the vengeance he had sought against Veloso and was making no attempt to hide the width of the gulf between them.

It was as if seeing her again he had been reminded she was a nobody, an illegitimate waif lifted from the streets of the city, owing whatever skills she did possess to the vested benevolence of a man he hated.

Once she had flagrantly disobeyed him. With a heart full of love she had left the apartment in search of a delicacy she could prepare and offer to him, since he appeared to want nothing else from her. If he hadn't understood her motives on that occasion, she wasn't going to explain them now—even if her lapse was to be held against her, together with all the other sins she had committed in his eyes.

'Perhaps I wasn't cut out for the life of a recluse.' The blonde waves danced on her shoulders, gleaming silver against the light. 'Perhaps now I've left the convent I want to spread my wings a little!' Blue eyes defied him to continue his neglect as Ria lied to support her pride.

'Do you think that's news to me?' His reply was like a slap in the face. 'But it was preferable for you to take your first flying lessons here in company with people I admire and trust, rather than fluttering out into the urban dangers of the city!' He raised a cynical eyebrow. 'I regret you found my friends and their parties so boring.'

She couldn't deny his assertion totally and he must have read the tacit agreement in the frankness of the gaze she turned on him, because his eyes narrowed thoughtfully as she plunged in to justify her reactions.

'I did like your friends, Vitor,' she told him honestly. 'They were charming and entertaining and amusing but— well,' she paused wishing she could tell from his expression how he was re-acting but it remained enigmatic. 'The fact is, I felt I wanted to do something more purposeful and serious with my time.'

'Indeed!' he retorted, more fiercely than her gentle mutiny deserved, Ria thought wretchedly. 'Well, we can't stand here discussing your future. We have to talk privately. Come back to the house.'

Ria bowed her head acquiescing to his command, feeling a sense of loss when he released her. There had been something ominous in his carefully modulated voice and she wasn't at all sure she wanted to hear what he had to say.

Vitor led her straight upstairs to the bedroom as a sad little smile played about her lips. Anyone seeing them would imagine they were about to indulge in a joyful reunion . . . unless that same someone had seen the dour expression on Vitor's face. Whatever he had in store for her, it wasn't an afternoon of love. That was one thing of which she could be quite certain!

Entering the room, she saw his suitcase standing on the floor, a large leather grip at its side. Her heart leapt. It seemed he intended a fairly long stay.

Ignoring the chairs in the room Ria sat on the bed to pull her riding-boots off before curling her legs beneath her as Vitor walked to the window to stand staring out across the paved patio with its subtropical plants and flowers. Patiently she waited for him to speak. When he did he seemed casual, almost detached.

'My parents have grown fond of you, Ria. They regard you as dearly as their own daughter.'

'I return their affection,' she told him quietly as he turned to rest his eyes on her anxious face. 'They—they're all the family I have.'

'No, Ria. That's not true any more,' he retorted swiftly, his voice hard-edged as she stared back at him completely nonplussed. 'You have an English grandfather, two aunts, numerous cousins.'

'What are you saying?' She was on her feet, her fingers digging into the skin of his upper arms as she tried to shake his firm masculine body in her agitation to know the truth. 'For God's sake tell me, Vitor. You can't have discovered my father.'

'Alas no. Your father is dead, *meu amor.*' He took her shaking hands and held them in his own. 'He was a very brave and clever man—a scientist working in the British Antarctic. His work was dangerous and top secret. When he was allowed a short leave he came to Brazil—a country he'd always loved. He met your mother and fell hopelessly in love with her.'

'Is this the truth?' She hardly breathed the words.

'Quite true, *meu amor.* Do you think I would lie to you?' For the first time he smiled and she responded by laying her head against his chest, feeling the thunder of his heart. His arms came round her enclosing her, strong and protective. 'It seems he saw your mother's father and asked permission to marry her. It was refused. He returned to the base camp promising to come back to her—but there was an accident—he was killed outright.'

'How do you know?' It was almost too much for Ria to take in. Yet Caterina had been right. Her lover had been prevented from returning to her. He hadn't willingly deserted her. After all these years she knew her mother's faith had been justified. Tears she hadn't been able to shed before spilled down her face.

'Friends in high places.' Vitor stroked her shining hair. 'I knew he was English, I knew his Christian names, I knew when he entered Brazil. Records showed when he left and where he went. The British authorities were very helpful when they heard your story. I was able to trace his family to a town in Dorset in England. Their name is Traveston. Your grandfather lives in a beautiful old English manor house not far from the coast. The whole family are very highly spoken of in the neighbourhood and appear to be quite wealthy.'

'You've been to England to see them?' Astounded Ria stared into his sombre face.

He nodded. 'It was in your interests I did so.'

'Oh, Vitor.' She didn't know what to say. She had been thinking him selfish and uncaring and he had actually been doing all this for her.

Very gently he released her hands, leaving her side to open the grip and extract a large package. 'Of course, you don't have to meet him if you don't want to, but your grandfather was overjoyed when he learned of your existence. You see, your father was his only son. To learn he had issue was a joy that brought him to tears. He wrote you a letter, Ria, and he's sent you photographs of your other relatives.' As she took the package from him with eager hands he added softly, 'He has also sent you his most treasured possession—the last letter he received from his son.'

'I don't understand how he could have accepted so readily that I was his granddaughter. Didn't he want proof?'

'He had all the proof he needed, Ria. I took him the photograph of your parents. The one you'd preserved so carefully in your Bible.'

'My Bible—but . . .'

'I always keep my promises, *menina*.' Vitor's fingers searched once more in the grip. When he returned to her he held her Bible and her rosary. 'I went to see Veloso before I left Brazil, and demanded my wife's belongings. The chauffeur had returned your case and it had been thrown aside in some box-room.'

'He didn't argue?' Ria shook her head in wonderment.

'Not after he'd taken my cheque in payment for the school fees he'd spent on you.'

'You gave him money for me?' Ria's voice quavered.

'I didn't want you beholden to him for anything.' He turned a burning gaze on her strained face. 'Don't you understand, Ria—there was no shame in my offering him money. The only shame was his—for accepting it!'

He turned away brusquely. 'You will want to read your grandfather's letter in peace. I mean to play the dutiful son for an hour or so and discuss the matters of the *fazenda* with Papa. We shall meet later at dinner.'

He had left the room without giving her a chance to express her gratitude. Ria was so full of emotion she didn't know whether to laugh or cry. She wanted so desperately to share her happiness with the man who had made it possible, but he had tossed his gift into her lap and departed without extending the opportunity to her.

She gave a deep sigh before sinking down slowly on the bed once more and opening the package. It was all there. Everything she had ever wanted to know.

Hours later Ria was walking alone through the pleasant gardens surrounding the *fazenda*, glad to be isolated with her own thoughts and memories, to breathe in the pleasant evening air, savouring its perfume, feeling its soft brush against her face.

Here it was autumn. In England it would be the beginning of spring. For years she had tried to imagine what her father's home must have been like. Now she knew. The package from her grandfather had included a multitude of colour photographs taken over the years in the pleasant English countryside around his house. She had looked at them so many times, she could recall how her relations looked—even recognise in their fairness a likeness to herself.

Her grandfather's letter had been a warm-hearted outpouring from a man whom she sensed instinctively she would be able to love. In it he had begged her and her husband to visit England. 'You have married a warm and generous man,' he had written. 'And I shall never cease to be grateful to him for the efforts he has made to bring me knowledge of your existence.'

The letter had made her weep, tears of utter happiness, but there had been the other letter too. Reading it she had sobbed out her heart, her face swollen and inflamed by the excess of her emotion. For Francis Bernard Traveston had written to his father about Caterina and his intentions to marry her. 'Be happy for me,' he had written. 'I have at last found the woman I cannot live without. Unfortunately her father is standing in our way but I'm sure true love will overcome all difficulties and it won't be too long before I'm able to bring Caterina home with me as my beloved wife.'

There had been more, but they were the words imprinted on Ria's mind. Reading them, she had cried with despair for the two wasted lives, the powerful love which had never been given the chance to mature, and she had cried for herself because she was married to a man who would never think of her in similar terms.

A quick glance at her watch warned her she would be late for dinner if she tarried where she was much longer. That would be unforgivable on Vitor's first night back after such a long absence.

Hurriedly she returned to the bedroom, saw that Vitor's case had been unpacked and presumed he had already gone downstairs. Showering quickly she donned a simple dress of apple green silk, straight-skirted, cowl-necked. It was a perfect foil for the bright fairness of her hair and the delicate sun-kissed skin of her shoulders. She applied make-up to her face, relieved to see that time had soothed the swollen tissues of her eyes and nose and that she appeared quite normal.

'My dearest girl.' Senhora Fortunato greeted her with outstretched arms as she entered the salon. 'Vitor has told us you have discovered your family.'

In the older woman's warm embrace, Ria looked over her shoulder to where Vitor stood, erect, expressionless, his eyes slowly taking in her appearance as if memorising every curve and hollow of her body.

'I have Vitor to thank for that. It was he who discovered who and where they were.' Her voice broke. 'It's difficult for me to put into words the way I feel.'

'I know how you feel. I can read it in your face.' Vitor came across, placing a casual arm round her waist, as Serena released her. 'But if you feel the need to put your feelings into words then by all means try—but over a good dinner.'

It was an excellent meal, although afterwards Ria couldn't even remember what she had eaten. She only knew it had tasted delicious, as had the white wine with which she washed it down. The entire conversation had centred around her newly discovered family, and as the wine had loosened her tongue she had found herself bubbling forth her happiness.

When Vitor suggested retiring early she was only too glad to comply, flinging herself down on the soft bed immediately she entered the room, stretching her slender body luxuriously and smiling up at Vitor as he came to sit beside her.

'This has been the happiest day of my life!' She reached her arms towards him, drawing his unresisting body into her arms and pressing the soft cheek against his own taut skin already darkening from the shadow of an incipient beard. 'I don't know how to thank you!'

She turned her mouth, feeling the harshness of his jaw against her tender flesh and pressed a breathless kiss on his skin, overwhelmed by a brimming affection.

Immediately she felt Vitor withdraw as his arms rejected her and he rose to his feet, striding to the window before speaking again.

'There's something you have to know. Your grandfather has offered you a permanent home in England, Ria.'

He wasn't even looking at her. Back turned, he was staring out into the velvet blackness of the Brazilian night.

Pain soared like an arrow through her heart.

'Permanent home?' There was a great lump in her throat. 'I don't understand. I have a permanent home here in Brazil with you!' Then as Vitor neither turned nor answered. 'Don't I, Vitor?' It was little more than a croak, and for a moment she wondered if it had penetrated the distance between them.

Then he spoke and she knew it had. 'Our marriage has served its purpose, *menina*. Believe me, I know how much Veloso is suffering both in body and spirit at this moment. To take you from him is the perfect punishment within the law for what he did.'

'And what did I do that I must be punished too?'

Vitor spun round at her agonised whisper.

'Nothing, Ria! I shall have to answer to God for what I subjected you to. I don't pretend my first intention wasn't revenge against Veloso, but I swear to you that if I hadn't truly believed what I did was also in *your* interest, I would have found another way. It was never my intention to hurt you or cause you grief. I know I must have frightened you and given you cause to hate me, but time was at a premium and you turned out to be more loyal and stubborn than I'd anticipated. I thought I was stealing a kitten and found I'd captured a brave and resourceful tigress!'

It was a fine declaration, but without foundation because at that moment he couldn't have hurt her more if he had taken his belt to her as she had once feared he might.

'And now you're sending me away, for ever?' With an almighty effort she kept her voice steady as she searched his tormented face.

'Sweet Ria.' He came to stand over her, lifting his hand to brush away the fine tendrils of hair that clung to her cheek. 'While you had no other home, this would have been yours. My family would have been your family—but—now you can be free to live your own life, make your own friends, find a man who loves you and one whose love you can return with all the passion of your pure little heart.'

His fingers trailed down her cheek, as, horrified at his words, she watched the painful path of his larynx as it moved in his golden throat.

'What are you saying to me?' she questioned hoarsely. '*You* are my husband, Vitor. We are married. How can you talk of another man?'

This couldn't be happening to her! She knew Vitor didn't love her, but she had never dreamed he meant to discard her, disown her. A cold terror clutched at her heart. Of course she wanted to meet her own family but not at the expense of her marriage. However sterile it was, it was all she had. She wanted to be with Vitor. Only in his presence did she achieve any sense of self-fulfillment.

'Our marriage can be annulled, Ria.' He spoke gently as if he were addressing the child he seemed to see her as. 'We've never lived together as man and wife.'

CHAPTER THIRTEEN

'No!' Somewhere Ria found the strength to oppose him. Scrambling off the bed, she evaded his grasp. 'No, that's not possible!'

His dark eyes met her furious blue ones. Before their pity she felt herself quail, reaching one hand back towards the wall to support herself. 'If one partner wilfully denies the other,' he began softly.

'I've never denied you anything!' It was a cry of despair. Wild thoughts chased through Ria's agonised brain. Suppose she threw herself at him now, tore off her clothes, offered herself, teased and tempted him until he made a mockery of the ground he had suggested? But she was too unsure, unpractised, to achieve what she wanted. He would laugh at her pathetic attempts, push her away. But there had to be some way to delay the moment of execution, something to give her a breathing space.

Vitor made an angry gesture with his hand. 'I know that. I didn't mean...'

He wasn't allowed to finish the sentence as, born of desperation, a wild solution occurred to Ria, stumbling off her tongue before she had had a chance to consider it deeply.

'In any case the marriage can't be annulled. I'm going to have a baby.'

She stood white and shaken, appalled at herself for lying, a wild heart-beating terror building up inside her as she looked at Vitor's astounded face.

This was how Lucifer must have looked when God had ordered him from heaven to a life of eternal hell. Horrified, proud, unbending and with a deep dark emptiness in his fine eyes which defied description but which promised a never-ending war of retribution.

Ria's hands rose protectively to hold her abdomen as if she was indeed sheltering a child beneath its firm warm walls.

When it seemed the silence would endure for ever Vitor said one word, 'Ricardo!'

'No! Oh, no, Vitor!' She'd lied unthinkingly. Stupidly she had never considered the way Vitor's mind would work. 'Not Ricardo!'

A cruel smile stretched his mouth, deepening the shadows beneath his cheek bones.

'Are you trying to tell me your pregnancy is parthenogenesis—that you managed it without the assistance of a male partner?'

Dumbly she shook her head, aware that beneath the quiet question a volcano of passion was building up within the strong hard frame of her husband.

'Well?' The single word demanded her confession.

'It was *you*, Vitor.' She saw the stupefaction on his face and plunged in deeper, ever deeper. 'That night when I'd left the apartment and you were so angry. Afterwards we ate and had a few drinks and then later when we went to bed...' Her eyes searched his face for a clue as to how he was receiving her story.

'Go on.' Softly he encouraged her. 'I don't remember anything of this.'

Ria dropped her eyes, staring down at her bare feet, her shoes long since discarded beneath the bed. In her desperation the story was coming easily to her lips. 'It was later—in the early hours of the morning—you were asleep, dreaming. You reached for me—touched me...'

She was improvising wildly, imagining how it might have been if he had truly loved and wanted her. 'You—you told me you loved me.'

There was nothing she could read on his enigmatic face. Emboldened by his silence she played her final card. 'You called me "Marta"—and then you—you...'

'Assaulted you?' he grated harshly.

'No!' Fiercely she rejected the suggestion. 'You made love to me.' She tossed back her mane of blonde hair and met his gaze without flinching. 'You wanted me and I wanted you—that's all there was to it!'

'Although I didn't even know who you were?' he asked softly.

'It didn't matter. We were man and wife. I didn't try to prevent it. It was right between us.'

She saw doubt now in the beloved face that regarded her, and pressed her advantage. Picking up her Bible from where it still lay on the bed, she held it to her heart.

'I've never been unfaithful to you, Vitor. I swear it!'

Endless aching seconds ticked away before Ria, unable to bear Vitor's silent scrutiny any longer, gave an aching sob of despair and flung herself face downwards on the bed.

She heard him move, felt the bed springs give beneath his weight, then his quiet voice echoed in her ears. 'I believe you, *querida*. Hush, don't cry so.' Light strong fingers stroked her hair, moved downwards to follow the line of her neck, gentle persuasive fingers that calmed the agitation that had made her whole body tremble. 'I'm sorry I can't remember what happened between us that night, *meu amor*. I must have been more affected by the wine than I'd supposed. Did I hurt you, frighten you?'

'No.' Ria swallowed, letting her imagination hold sway, telling him how she had wanted it to be between them. 'You were so gentle, Vitor, so tender.'

'And passionate too, I hope?'

She heard the smile in his voice and knew then that it was going to be all right. 'Yes,' she said. 'Oh, yes.' Her voice dreamy, she raised her head from the pillow and turned her eyes, shining with love, to meet his dark regard.

'Did I kiss you like this, *namorada*?' His mouth found hers, parted her eager lips and discovered no barrier to its quest. 'Did I touch you like this, Ria? Here? And here?' His hand moved, fingers splayed. The sure, loving touch of a man who knows the soft female flesh that thrilled beneath him was welcoming him.

Ria moaned, turning on the bed so that he could pull down the zip of her dress to drag the unresisting silk from her warm pulsating body. Beneath it she wore only a pale matching camisole. As Vitor's fingers pushed the thin straps away it was Ria who touched her own body, offering her breasts to his mouth, giving short ecstatic gasps as he buried his face in their pale loveliness, tasting their perfumed beauty, bringing them to a sweet fruition between his lips, worshipping their perfection until she thought she could bear it no longer.

Blindly Ria reached for the man she loved, found his shirt-covered shoulders and removed the fine cotton with urgent fingers, pulling at the neck, feeling the buttons give and caring nothing save that she could feel the quickening male flesh warm and musky shuddering to her touch.

When Vitor's hand slid down her silky skin, leaving a trail of caresses as it journeyed, she was ready for him. She heard his gasp of understanding and her own answering moan of deprivation as for a few moments he rolled away. Then he was kneeling over her, positioning her with hungry capable hands to ensure her comfort, spreading her body to receive his own without pain or stress.

There was a brief moment when, gazing awestruck at his aroused body, Ria felt fear. Her biology lessons at the convent had never prepared her for the sheer majestic power of the virile male. In comparison she felt small and inadequate. Suppose she should disappoint him— be unable to accept him as she so desperately wanted to? Because of her lie, he didn't even know this was the first time for her.

'My sweet love.' His face flushed across his cheekbones, Vitor spoke hoarsely, each word articulated with great effort. There were beads of sweat on his upper lip— on the wide brow. 'Don't be frightened, *meu amor*. Trust me, *querida*...'

As if by magic every trace of apprehension drained from her. Her whole being relaxed as her body rose to meet his approach and they became joined, welded together, forged into the perfect union in the universal fire of love.

No one had told her it was like this. Like a bird fluttering against the bars of a cage Ria was desperate to be free, to find her wings, to soar away from the world— just she and Vitor. But when release came she took it alone, believing in that extended fraction of time that she was facing a kind of death and going willingly to meet it.

Somewhere on another plane she could hear her own voice: hear the cadence of half-spoken phrases tumbling from her own mouth: but could make no sense of them.

Weightless and alone, she heard Vitor cry out a deep shuddering groan that brought her back to reality in time to feel the full weight of his body collapse against her, then ease away as his face pressed against her neck and he breathed great sawing gasps. Wrapping her arms around him, her own breathing none too steady, she held him tightly as she might a child and waited for the storm to subside.

Savouring each moment of his quiescent nearness, she trailed loving fingers across his satiated flesh, hoping against hope he might sleep the deep slumber of fulfilment in her arms so that she might not be called on to account for the wild fabrication she had devised to ensnare him—or at least not until the morning so that she could keep the memory of one perfect night for ever in her memory.

She felt him stir against her and knew her unuttered prayer was to remain unanswered.

'Tell me, Ria. Look me in the eyes and let me hear you say it.' Raised on one elbow, Vitor demanded her response, his eyes brilliantly dark in the moonlit room as insistent as the husky undertones of his voice.

Ria met those piercing eyes without flinching, determined to meet this moment of truth with as much dignity as she was capable of dredging up. 'I lied to you, Vitor. No man ever touched me before tonight—let alone you.' She swallowed hard, trying to dispel the hard pain that constricted her throat. 'I'm sorry.'

It was no lie. She was sorry, because love couldn't be stolen any more than it could be bought and, for those few ecstatic moments of absolute pleasure, she might have turned his tolerance of her to hatred. She wanted to add—'forgive me'—but what man would be able to absolve a woman who had lied about carrying his child in order to trap him into continuing a marriage he didn't want?

Instead, she clenched her jaw, preparing herself to feel the lash of his tongue, the scythe of his scorn, perhaps even the flat of his hand across her face.

All she heard was a soft laugh. 'No, that wasn't what I meant. What I want to hear is what you told me over and over again a few moments ago. This time I want to see your face when you say it—watch your lips form the words that you cried out repeatedly when I took your body and made it mine.'

Yes, she remembered it now. The wild tumbling words that had sprung like a gusher from the well of her heart, stripping her soul as naked as Vitor had already stripped her body. Trembling, still uncertain as to his motives, she obeyed him.

'I love you, Vitor,' she whispered, her tone wavering, then firming as to her wonderment she saw deep satisfaction smooth the hard bones of his face. 'I love you, I love you!' Tears spilled from her eyes as Vitor gathered her into his arms, comforting her with soft kisses on her face, stroking her hair, murmuring a soft lover's litany of endearments.

Remorse made her voice thick and husky as she buried her tear-damp face against Vitor's strong neck. 'I couldn't bear to be sent away—to be written out of your life. I'd rather stay with you unloved than have half the world between us. That's why I told that awful, awful lie.'

'A fabrication that never fooled me for one moment, *namorada*!' Laughter deepened his reply as Ria raised her solemn face to meet his tender regard. 'Only an innocent woman could imagine for one instant that a man could make love to her in his sleep and have no knowledge of it.'

Ria's mouth turned into a wry smile. That was a mistake she would never make again—not after tonight!

'Besides which,' he continued inexorably, 'if I had been dreaming of *anyone* in my sleep, it would have been *you*, my sweet Ria—not Marta.'

'But you loved her, Vitor.' Ria was quick to acknowledge the other woman's place in his heart and his life.

'Yes, I did,' he agreed simply. 'But not in the way you obviously believe.' He gave a deep sigh, seemingly collecting his thoughts while Ria waited silently, sensing he had a need to talk about the woman who had played such a major role in his history. Her patience was soon rewarded as he started to speak again.

'I was just twenty-seven when I met her—arrogant and self-centred. The only son of a wealthy farmer who demanded respect and obedience but who was prepared to indulge me where the pleasures of the flesh were concerned. Consequently I grew up with a distorted view of life, believing money could buy me everything I wanted—friends, entertainment, good food and wine...women. Of course, I knew in theory the problems of the northeast, but they hadn't seemed relevant to my life-style—and then I met Marta. It was she who opened my eyes to what was really going on outside my privileged circle. Really opened them.

'She was strong-minded, forceful and determined with an inner beauty that was compelling. I was completely bowled over by her intelligence and her oratory. I gave up everything here in São Paolo and went up north with her, using whatever skills I had to help the people who needed them rather than just the people who were able to pay for them.'

'Oh, my dear love.' Ria responded to his pain by leaning forward and placing a soft kiss on the smooth skin of his shoulder.

'When she was killed I knew I had to avenge her memory. It was a personal debt for our friendship. Veloso can't be hurt by fines. He's too clever to risk being jailed. Physical retribution was out of the question since it would betray the humanist ideals which were Marta's code. So I set about finding a weakness, an Achilles' heel where I could pierce his thick hide; and thanks to Luisa I discovered you—the lovely young girl he'd earmarked for his own enjoyment.

'The simplest way of making sure you never reached Veloso's house was to waylay you on the final stage of your journey. The apartment in São Paolo had belonged to Marta. She was a childless widow and, much to my astonishment, she'd made me her heir. It was poetic justice to marry you and take you back there.'

'She was very lovely,' Ria interrupted softly. 'That night when her photo fell from the bed and you asked her to forgive you I...'

'You thought we were lovers?' Astonishment echoed in the question as Vitor held her away from him to stare down at her raised face. 'My darling, that photo was taken when Marta was a young woman. When I first met her she was over fifty. Lovely still, but, believe me, I was only ever her protégé in a good cause.'

'Oh!' For a few seconds Ria was lost for words. No one had spoken of Marta's age, and she had simply assumed the photo to be a current one. 'But—but you apologised to her for—for——'

'For being on the point of behaving like an animal?' Bitterness tinged his angry retort. 'Because Marta had taught me the true meaning of machismo. That it has nothing to do with appearance or wealth, but everything to do with honour and dignity, with protection of the weak. It isn't enough to look like a man, one must act like a man—exercise responsibility, acknowledge obligation—and I was on the point of forgetting it all. Dear God, I wanted you so badly, it was tearing me apart!'

'But I wanted you too, Vitor—with all your experience of women, couldn't you tell?' All her abundant feelings for him shone in her luminous eyes.

'You'll never know how much I tried to make myself believe that.' A sad smile accompanied the confession. 'But you were my wife, and you'd been taught a wife's duties were to obey her husband. I didn't want obedience. I wanted love. And I wasn't going to settle for anything less. You see, Ria, that night I was forced to admit to myself what I'd been fighting against almost since the first time I saw you. I was in love with you. Never before had I known the torment and jealousy such a state can make a man suffer.'

Love? It had been *love* that had roused Vitor to such a passion—not anger at her disobedience?

'But you were furious with me,' she protested.

'Of course I was! And justifiably so. I come back unexpectedly, and find you've disappeared. All kinds of horrific thoughts besiege me; I imagine you taken by force, involved in an accident, robbed, raped—even murdered!

'Then you walk in as if nothing is untoward. One look at your face and you're no longer the schoolgirl whose very innocence and ingenuity had been her protection. A few strokes of pencil and brush and you are transformed into a beautiful woman. *Meu Deus,* Ria! The pitiful self-deception I'd been practising was ripped away and I was forced to face the truth. Not only did I love you for what you were—unspoiled and honest and very, very brave, but I wanted you, desired you in the way a man desires a woman, with every cell of my body and fibre of my being!' He gave a brief laugh. 'And that had never been a part of my plan!'

'Because of my background?' Safe now in the knowledge he had overcome such scruples Ria found she could ask the question without pain. 'I was just an urchin—no wonder you were ashamed of wanting me!'

'Stop it, you sweet fool!' Vitor's hand twisted in her hair, bringing her face to within inches of his own so she couldn't escape the blazing fury of his dark eyes. 'Do you think I cared one whit about your background? Who you were was nothing to me—only what you were— and what I'd done to you. I'd saved you from one prison only to place you in another. I had no right to keep you shackled to my side unwillingly. To do so was to reduce myself to Veloso's level. You were fortune's fool—an unwilling victim of fate. I had to preserve your innocence, find a safe and welcoming place for you—and let you go!'

A wry smile twisted his lips. 'So I tried to convince myself you were only a child, forced myself to treat you like one—even kept calling you *menina* as a crude reminder to my baser nature that you were not for me!' He groaned as if ashamed at his own weakness. 'But I failed abysmally, *meu amor*. I only had to look into your beautiful eyes to remember that they'd seen atrocities that had robbed you of your childhood for ever and you were all the woman any man could dare to hunger for! In the end there was only one way I could alleviate the pain of living with you and not becoming your lover— I had to put some distance between us.'

As if the very thought of losing her was too much to bear, Vitor closed the gap between them, taking her mouth, enfolding her naked body to his own, lying down on the bed and pulling her down on top of him.

'Oh, Vitor...' The break in Ria's voice belied the joy in her face as she gazed at him with adoring, dark-pupilled eyes. 'How can I ever find the words to tell you how much it means to me knowing I have a family of my own—people who want to meet me—welcome me...'

'I told you not to lose your faith in miracles,' Vitor reminded her, a throb of emotion making his deep voice tremble. 'I love you so dearly I would have spent a fortune and a lifetime, if necessary, to wipe out the suffering you were caused that night, and to fulfil your deepest dreams, *querida*.'

'I had no idea.' Ria could have cursed her own blindness. 'When you went away so abruptly, I was certain it was because you couldn't stand the sight of me,' she confessed. 'I thought I was being punished.'

'No—if anyone was being made to suffer it was me,' Vitor told her softly. 'Deliberately choosing to stay away from your side so that you could enjoy a broad aspect of life—mix with people your own age—and discover a future from which I was determined to exclude myself—for your own good.'

'I want to see my family more than anything else in the world—except to stay here with you.' When she could speak again Ria enforced the meaning of her attestation by running her soft mouth across Vitor's face, relaxed now in the sweet aftermath of love. 'I was so terrified when I thought you were going to get our marriage declared void, I think I went a little mad. I thought if I could persuade you I was bearing your child, not only would it destroy any grounds for annulment, but you might be prepared to let me stay with you.' She shuddered deeply. 'Afterwards, when it was so obvious I'd invented the whole thing—I thought you might be so furious at my deception you would kill me!'

Vitor gave a rueful laugh. 'I could easily have done just that when you first told me you were pregnant. I was already burning with jealousy after seeing you and Ricardo so happy together—even though I knew he was only doing what I'd asked of him. For a moment I thought my world had blown up in my face... and then reason took over from fury; because I loved you both I knew neither of you would have deceived me with the other.

'That seemed to leave only one other explanation— that you wanted to stay married to me after all. That you loved me.' His loving hands touched her with exquisite, mind-searing possession apparent in each predatory finger. '...*querida* Ria...all you had to do was tell me!'

Ria made a little moue. 'You didn't make it easy for me, Vitor,' she protested in mock indignation. 'There were Felicia and Marta—or at least I thought there were,' she amended.

She felt the gliding passage of his firm hands following the warm curves of her body invoking a trail of delight in their wake. 'Felicia was socially suitable, but there was never any real feeling on either side. It was my lucky day when she rejected me. And as for making it easy for you—from now on I'm going to devote my life to doing just that!' He smiled lovingly into her heart-shaped face, drinking in the dewy freshness of her lovely mouth, the irresistible feminine scent of her skin. 'Even an embryo politician is allowed some time for play, and I've always had a yearning to stay in England in the spring. And afterwards, when we return, I'll sell the apartment and we'll buy a house with a garden and swimming-pool in one of the garden suburbs of São Paolo so that you and the children can live in beautiful surroundings and return the hospitality of your English family.'

'But Vitor,' she protested urgently. 'I'm not pregnant!'

'How can you possibly be sure of that, *meu amor*?' He kissed her very gently, his handsome face alight with an almost boyish mischief. 'And even if you're not, there's no guarantee you won't be soon.'

'No, I suppose not.' Ria's mouth curled into a self-satisfied smile as she lifted herself slightly, allowing the hard, passionate mouth of the man she loved to seek and nurture the rosy crowns of her pale breasts.

'And because I'm a jealous husband and an ardent lover who intends to demand my wife's sole attention for many hours of each day, I wondered if you'd like to ask your Aunt Luisa to take on the role of nanny, hmm?'

'Could I? Oh, could I?' She thought she had got her tears under control, but the fresh evidence of Vitor's thoughtfulness caught her off guard. Hastily she wiped away the dampness on her lashes. 'She loves children...'

'I know.' His tone was quietly amused. 'At the moment she's acting as nanny to the children of the manager at the farm where you and I first spent the night together. I wasn't going to risk Veloso's kitchen becoming too hot for her! I believe she's being quite well paid, but I dare say we could bribe her away if, and when, you want to.'

'I've been so worried about her,' Ria admitted honestly. 'But I dared not try to make contact in the circumstances.'

'I know.' Vitor's quiet response was more telling than a thousand words, as it acknowledged the total sympathetic unity between them which was the product of their mutual love.

Ria sighed blissfully. She would no longer be alone, unlike Heitor Olvidades, locked in the cold prison of his own intolerance. An incredible feeling of wonder suddenly flooded through her. In that brief instant when her mind had touched on the memory of her maternal grandfather, she had felt no bitterness—only a passing sadness that in his old age he would be, from his own choice, alone and unloved, when she had so much.

Humbly she recognised her discovery as being yet another miracle. Pity had displaced hatred in her heart, and Caterina's last wish had found fulfilment. Heitor Olvidades' granddaughter had been given the grace to forgive him.

Minutes later Ria felt the quickening of Vitor's lithe male body and as he turned with her and over her, a lover's litany of adoration pouring unrestrainedly from his passionate lips, she sighed her pleasure and surrendered herself completely to him.

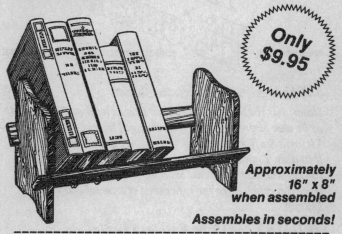

*Exciting, adventurous, sensual stories
of love long ago*

On Sale Now:

SATAN'S ANGEL by Kristin James

*Slater was the law in a land that was as wild and untamed
as he was himself, but all that changed when he met
Victoria Stafford. She had been raised to be a lady, but
that didn't mean she had no will of her own. Their search
for her kidnapped cousin brought them together, but they
were too much alike for the course of true love to run
smooth.*

PRIVATE TREATY by Kathleen Eagle

*When Jacob Black Hawk rescued schoolteacher
Carolina Hammond from a furious thunderstorm, he
swept her off her feet in every sense of the word, and she
knew that he was the only man who would ever make her
feel that way. But society had put barriers between them
that only the most powerful and overwhelming love could
overcome...*

Look for them wherever Harlequin books are sold.

Temptation™

TEMPTATION WILL BE
EVEN HARDER TO RESIST...

In September, Temptation is presenting a sophisticated new face to the world. A fresh look that truly brings Harlequin's most intimate romances into focus.

What's more, all-time favorite authors Barbara Delinsky, Rita Clay Estrada, Jayne Ann Krentz and Vicki Lewis Thompson will join forces to help us celebrate. The result? A very special quartet of Temptations...

- **Four striking covers**
- **Four stellar authors**
- **Four sensual love stories**
- **Four variations on one spellbinding theme**

All in one great month! Give in to Temptation in September.

Coming in April

Harlequin Category Romance Specials!

Look for six new and exciting titles from this mix of two genres.

4 Regencies—lighthearted romances set in England's Regency period (1811-1820)

2 Gothics—romance plus suspense, drama and adventure

Regencies

Daughters Four by Dixie Lee McKeone
She set out to matchmake for her sister, but reckoned without the Earl of Beresford's devilish sense of humor.

Contrary Lovers by Clarice Peters
A secret marriage contract bound her to the most interfering man she'd ever met!

Miss Dalrymple's Virtue by Margaret Westhaven
She needed a wealthy patron—and set out to buy one with the only thing she had of value....

The Parson's Pleasure by Patricia Wynn
Fate was cruel, showing her the ideal man, then making it impossible for her to have him....

Gothics

Shadow over Bright Star by Irene M. Pascoe
Did he want her shares to the silver mine, her love—or her life?

Secret at Orient Point by Patricia Werner
They seemed destined for tragedy despite the attraction between them....

Lynda Ward's

LEAP THE MOON

...the continuing saga of *The Welles Family*

You've already met Elaine Welles, the oldest daughter of powerful tycoon Burton Welles, in Superromance #317, *Race the Sun*. You cheered her on as she threw off the shackles of her heritage and won the love of her life, Ruy de Areias.

Now it's her sister's turn. Jennie Welles is the drop-dead-gorgeous, most rebellious Welles sister, and she's determined to live life her way—and flaunt it in her father's face.

When she meets Griffin Stark, however, she learns there's more to life than glamour and independence. She learns about kindness, compassion and sharing. One nagging question remains: is she good enough for a man like Griffin? Her father certainly doesn't think so....

Leap the Moon...a Harlequin Superromance coming to you in August. Don't miss it!